THE SUMMER OF LOVE

The sixties are swinging — but not so much for young fashion shop owner Joanie. All she needs is love, though it's not forthcoming where her mother is concerned. Only the aunt who Joanie lives with seems to care for her. Then she meets Martin, an airline pilot, who shows her love she can respond to — yet he's not all he appears to be. But then Joanie has her own secrets too. It will take a near-tragedy before matters are resolved . . .

JOHN DARLEY

◆

THE SUMMER OF LOVE

Complete and Unabridged

LINFORD
Leicester

First published in Great Britain in 2020

First Linford Edition
published 2022

A catalogue record for this book is available
from the British Library.

ISBN 978-1-4448-4920-2

Published by
Ulverscroft Limited
Anstey, Leicestershire

Printed and bound in Great Britain by
TJ Books Ltd., Padstow, Cornwall

This book is printed on acid-free paper

Dead End Street

Stepping off the bus as it pulled into Hillford's unassuming terminus, Jean — now Joanie Saunders — suddenly experienced a feeling of both apprehension and despair. This was in sharp contrast to her usual fairly carefree attitude towards life.

The slim, fair, twenty-two-year-old slung her rucksack over one shoulder and, taking a deep breath, set off in the bright April sunlight towards 23 Setford Avenue, an address she hadn't been back to since her early childhood.

She'll always be your mother, Jean, you must remember that. The words of her aunt — the person who she really thought of as her mother — came back to Joanie now as, with each hesitant, reluctant step she drew nearer to her destination.

As she walked, she looked about her, noticing that a lot had changed — even here, despite the sleepy Sunday atmosphere.

The Sixties were in full swing as was constantly in evidence in Chepswell, the suburb of London where Joanie ran her boutique — with the help of Aunt Mary's generous financial contributions.

It had been hard at first but now, gradually, Joanie was establishing a reputation for herself as both an entrepreneur and designer in her own right.

Four years at art college had given her that right and the practical ability.

It was there, also, that she decided to become Joanie instead of Jean. Jean by definition was misleading, Joanie was much more innovative and avant garde. And it was also, for some reason, liberating.

And then, soon after her twenty-first birthday she changed her surname from Monckton to Saunders, her aunt's name. It somehow seemed more appropriate, despite Aunt Mary's slight misgivings at her not informing her mother of the change.

But all that seemed irrelevant at this moment. Her hand on the gate of number 23, she had to grip it very tightly to prevent herself from turning away and running back to where constancy, security and, above all, love could claim her.

She had lost all confidence and composure, wishing so much to be at work where things made sense and had a purpose.

'I need to see you, I can't explain over the telephone. You will come, won't you?'

It had been a rhetorical question; she'd known that Joanie would go. Despite everything, there was still this physical, blood connection which could not be undone. And now here she was — although not quite.

The gate was as much an obstacle as an opening. How long she might have remained there she would never know because, at that moment, the front door opened and a figure — unfamiliar yet so well known — appeared at the door and beckoned her in.

Reflections

Joanie had never known her father. He had been killed during the Normandy invasion. Joanie's mother had been devastated by the news and was in no way compensated by the fact that she was carrying her husband's child.

When Joanie was born, in early February 1945, Celia Monckton still could not feel any sort of bonding affection towards her daughter. She was constantly assured that she would feel differently in time but it never happened.

She would not even feed her baby and eventually Joanie became the responsibility of Celia's elder sister.

This proved to be a good arrangement, sparing Joanie from her mother's acute depression and, sometimes, odd behaviour.

Over the years Joanie would only see her mother when she — Celia, that is — deemed it necessary. It would not be on any particular occasion — a birthday, say, or a school festival — but just as and when the mood took her.

Their relationship never developed, however. Joanie was shy of her, and Celia Monckton's attitude towards her daughter was icily cool.

That made it all the more mysterious and slightly unnerving that she would want to see Joanie now, especially in the home she'd never known. Joanie's initial reluctance to go was listened to and understood by her aunt — she had no-one else she could turn to.

It had always remained a sort of a secret as to the circumstances surrounding her absent mother. Only Aunt Mary understood and could give advice worth heeding.

'You'd better go, dear,' she'd said. 'She may have changed. People do.'

'But why now? Why so suddenly?' Joanie could imagine a gradual evolving of emotions over time. But this?

'It's not as if she wanted things to be as they are,' Aunt Mary continued. 'In her heart I'm sure she loves you. It just got buried in the avalanche of sadness when your father died.'

'But that's not my fault. And what could she possibly have to tell me that would matter to me?'

'Well, I just think you're going to have to go and find that out, dear.'

Puppet on a String

Joanie's eyes remained focused on the tiled pathway as she made her way towards the open front door of this suburban semi-detached house, aware that her mother was all the while staring fixedly at her.

'Hello, Jean,' she said, stepping back so that her daughter could enter.

'Hello.'

Both were aware of an awkwardness between them which a quick hug or kiss might have helped to alleviate.

'We are in the sitting-room, come through.'

Joanie was alarmed to hear her mother use the word 'we'. Who could the 'we' possibly be?

She was about to find out.

From the spacious hall, Joanie followed Celia Monckton into what Aunt Mary would call the front room. On entering, Joanie's mother stepped aside.

'Henry, this is Jean, my daughter,' she

said. 'Jean, Henry Smythe.'

With the sun streaming in through the large bay window, Joanie was aware only, at first, of a silhouetted shape standing in the centre of the room. As her eyes struggled to adjust, the figure moved towards her and the silhouette slowly dissolved, revealing a tall, slimmish man in his late forties or early fifties, perhaps, his hand outstretched and a pleasant smile on a not unattractive smooth-skinned face.

'How do you do, Jean. Very pleased to meet you.'

Joanie accepted his greeting, and accepted, too, for the time being, their use of the name she no longer answered to. But once the hand shaking was done there seemed nothing else to say. There was no 'I've heard so much about you' from either party.

Joanie imagined this meeting was as much of a surprise to Henry as it was to herself.

'I've made tea,' Celia said. 'Henry, perhaps you could wheel the trolley in for me. It's in the kitchen.'

Henry duly set off to fetch the trolley, leaving mother and daughter standing self-consciously opposite one another in the comfortably furnished room.

'Do sit down, Jean. Make yourself at home.'

Celia attempted to smile as she herself now sat down. Joanie noticed a lack of composure in her mother's manner, something she'd never seen before.

I wonder what she's got to be nervous about, she wondered.

And then Henry reappeared, all smiles, with the trolley.

Strangers in the Night

Joanie had booked ahead a room at Hillford's one and only local hotel. Why would anyone want to stay here, if they didn't live here, she had often asked herself. She wanted, more than anything, to get back on a bus and head home as quickly as possible.

She had initially booked a room because she suspected — or even hoped — that her mother was going to tell her something that might be a catalyst in bringing the two of them closer together.

Her shop was never open on a Monday so at least there would be time for both parties to begin the process of repatriation, as it were. But the news she was presented with was both shocking and astonishing in one fell swoop, and was almost certainly guaranteed to drive an even greater wedge between them.

It was the matter-of-fact casualness of it all which shocked — and hurt —

Joanie. Her mother might have been telling her that they were going to get a new car or vacuum cleaner.

'Henry and I are getting married, Jean,' she'd said, and didn't seem at all interested in Joanie's response. She proceeded to pour out the three cups of tea.

'I think we shall need more hot water, Henry, if you please,' she'd added, as if she was not actually in the least bit interested in what Joanie might have to say regarding her news.

Joanie had stayed as long as she politely could, even raising a small glass of sherry in their honour. But when she started to offer excuses for leaving, Henry intervened.

'Oh dear, that's a shame. My son's due to arrive soon. I was hoping you would meet him.'

'He doesn't know yet, either,' Celia added, implying, it would seem, that Joanie had been privileged to be the first to be told their news.

'I'm sorry, I have to go, I'm afraid . . . work and such. Sorry.'

And then she'd left without further explanation, desperate to put as much distance between herself and the happy couple as was humanly possible.

Distance, she thought. How ironic. As if there wasn't enough distance, emotionally, between her and her mother. Guiltily she acknowledged that Henry whatever his name was — Smythe, was it? — had seemed quite genuinely friendly.

Perhaps he could sense the atmosphere and aloofness caused by Joanie's mother's apparent indifference to her own flesh and blood and wanted to introduce a bit of warmth and humanity to the proceedings. But it would be an uphill struggle.

Joanie had tried — and failed — all her life. What she found particularly hurtful was how her mother could offer love and affection to this man and yet not to her. It appeared there was a seam of such feelings that existed somewhere in her heart, but only enough for Henry.

★ ★ ★

After a quick shower in her en-suite, Joanie started to feel a little better, and a little hungry too. She changed into a top and skirt which she had designed and made herself and then went down, first of all to the bar, to get herself a much-needed glass of wine.

It was as she was turning, with her glass, from the bar, that a man, young, well built, handsome — all these things she somehow managed to spot just before he collided with her, spilling her wine.

'Oh, I am so sorry!' the young man said, the dark tone of his voice adding to Joanie's feeling of attraction, ridiculous as it was.

'No need to apologise,' she said, finding herself somewhat hypnotised by his almost radiant blue eyes which continued to gaze into hers.

'I think I might just go and change my skirt, though.'

There was an awkward moment as they both sidestepped the wrong way.

'Sorry,' the young man said again. Then he stopped wavering, standing resolutely in front of her.

'Are you staying here?' he asked. Joanie nodded.

'Great,' he continued, 'then let me invite you to dinner. They have quite a cosmopolitan menu here for an old English hotel. What do you say?' His eyes sparkled as he smiled, and Joanie felt a glow of warmth suffuse her. How could she refuse?

'Thank you, but there's really no need,' she said weakly.

A matter of minutes later they were both seated opposite one another in the Tudor beamed restaurant that had once been the saloon bar.

'I'm Martin,' the young man said, reaching across to shake Joanie's hand. 'Martin Smith.'

There was an almost imperceptible hesitation as he told her his full name, as if the commonness of the surname caused him some sort of vague embarrassment.

Joanie took his hand, at the same time revealing her own name. After this a moment's awkwardness occurred, but, fortunately the waiter appeared to take their orders.

A couple of glasses of wine later, plus the delicious starter and their initial shyness had worn off as they started to get to know each other.

'So you are a fashion designer,' Martin said, obviously impressed. 'And with your own shop, too. That's just amazing.'

'Well, being a pilot is pretty impressive, too,' Joanie countered, with a grin. They were getting on famously, and seemed to share so many interests.

Martin had described how his job as a pilot with BOAC took him all over the world.

'Trouble is, you tend to miss out on what this country has to offer,' he said.

'I don't think Hillford has much to offer.' Joanie smiled.

Martin frowned.

'So what brings you here, then?'

Now it was Joanie's turn to frown.

'Oh, just family stuff,' she hedged. 'What are you going to have for your main course?' she added, a little more light-heartedly than she suddenly was feeling, as the memory of her mother's announcement earlier intruded on her present enjoyment.

Martin, sensing Joanie's unease, turned to the menu, and for the next few minutes they were both seemingly absorbed in choosing what they would eat as their main course.

However, they were both also considering — and hoping — that this chance encounter might yet develop into something more, perhaps.

The evening was a success and, for Joanie, it deadened the hurt that her mother had caused her with her news.

'It would be great if we could meet up again,' Martin said, those captivating eyes of his silently expressing just how much he would like that.

'That would be nice. Here's my contact number,' she said, taking one of her cards from her bag.

'Oh . . . er . . . great,' he said. 'Have you got another one of these that I could write my own contact details on, for you?' he added. 'I live in London, too. Sadly I don't run to a business card though.'

Joanie, feeling the colour rush to her cheeks, scrambled about unnecessarily in her bag, finally producing another card for Martin.

To her mind, things were seeming to go off course. There was a touch of formality and restraint edging back into what had been an enjoyable evening.

Martin produced a very elegant fountain pen from the inside pocket of his jacket and then, with an equally elegant hand, wrote his details on to the back of Joanie's card.

He waved it about for a few seconds for it to dry, looking about him self-consciously as he did so. Once satisfied that it would not smudge, he handed it back to Joanie, standing up as he did so.

'I have to get back to London, Joanie. I've really enjoyed this evening.' He reached out his hand and for some peculiar reason it gave Joanie a sense of déjà vu.

She realised that that's how the evening had begun — with a handshake — but this feeling had nothing to do with that, and it left her with a sense of unease long after Martin had left.

Happy Together

Back home, back at work, Joanie soon gave up wondering about Martin, her mother and all the other things which kept her awake that Sunday night into the early hours of Monday morning at Hillford. When she'd told her aunt — not about meeting Martin but about her mother's announcement — Mary Saunders's response was one of contained surprise.

'It's a good thing she wanted to share her news with you, Joanie. That must mean something. Will you go to the wedding?'

Joanie sighed.

'I haven't been invited yet. I'll just see what happens. It's all a bit weird.'

Mary frowned at her niece's choice of word to describe the situation but said no more.

When an invitation did come, however, it wasn't from Celia Monckton but from Martin. He telephoned Joanie at the shop, wondering if it would be all right to come over and see her.

'Yes, of course,' Joanie said, secretly more delighted than her voice was suggesting.

'I don't suppose you close for lunch but perhaps I could get us something locally. There's bound to be a deli somewhere, is there?'

There was indeed a deli locally and, before arriving at Joanie's boutique, Martin had called in and bought a few items which he hoped would serve as lunch for them both.

'I love the name,' he said, as he came into the shop. 'Al La Mod. I get it, absolutely.'

Joanie smiled.

'It's not quite so up to date any more, but people have got to know it so it doesn't seem to matter.'

They went through to the back room where Joanie designed, made or altered the clothes for which she was beginning to establish a reputation for herself.

'I'll just clear a space,' she said.

'Please, don't go to any trouble. I hope I haven't disrupted your day. I don't suppose you normally close for lunch, do you?'

She didn't — but it didn't seem to matter, for once. Besides, she'd covered herself by putting a note on the door for anyone to ring the bell if they really wanted to come in.

Having settled themselves in the two not altogether comfortable chairs, and with the kettle steaming up on the table behind, they spent a few minutes enjoying the repast that Martin had brought for them.

'This ham is delicious,' Joanie acknowledged. 'I usually skip lunch or maybe have a couple of biscuits with my coffee.'

'I'm glad you're enjoying it.' Martin smiled, and there was that sensation of warmth coupled with anticipated excitement which Joanie could not help but experience.

'Have you been to any exotic destinations since we last met?' Joanie said, trying to normalise things, along with her feelings.

'Well, nothing comes close to Hillford, obviously.'

'Obviously.' They both laughed. It struck her as bizarre how a place which, until recently, she had only had bad associations with, could have become so easily a source of amusement. It was as if, since meeting Martin, a whole lot of tension in her was gradually unwinding. She was feeling relaxed and, for some reason, optimistic.

'I'm off to Portugal tomorrow but after I come back I've got a week's leave due. I was wondering whether we might spend a bit more time together — go to the pictures perhaps?'

Joanie had already said yes, in her mind, before Martin had even finished asking.

'I'd like that,' she said. 'I'd like that very much.'

After Martin had left, Joanie got back into the work routine; selling, advising, altering, all the while buoyed up by how she was feeling with regard to Martin.

She had no real justification for feeling this way; Martin might just be looking for someone to pass the time with — to fill a gap — between whatever romantic liaisons his travels afforded him.

But despite these slightly nagging thoughts, she kept them well at the back of her mind, determined to enjoy the prospect of spending time with such a good-looking guy, whatever his own agenda might be.

* * *

'You seem particularly cheerful, dear,' Mary observed, as they sat down for supper. 'Had a good day in the shop?'

'I had a very good day in the shop, actually.' Joanie grinned, going on to describe Martin's visit.

'He sounds a very agreeable young man.' Mary nodded. 'And a pilot, no less. How romantic.'

Mary's use of out of date expressions and her love of romance often caused speculation in Joanie's mind as to whether there had ever been an 'agreeable young man' in her aunt's life. She would love to know more about her family's past, especially as it was a dead end as far as her mother was concerned. But, as much as she cared for her aunt, there would never be that sort of intimacy between them that might allow such personal matters to be discussed.

I know as little about the past as I do about the future, she thought, although, as regards the future, she felt there were definite signs that it was something to look forward to.

The First Cut is the Deepest

Late spring and early summer were always particularly busy times for Joanie but they were also times when she needed to take stock of her range and make a study of coming trends.

Many of the magazines helped her with this but, of course, there was no substitute for seeing for yourself. So, what she would do, as on this particular Monday in early May, was to take herself off to the West End and do a bit of market research.

She would set herself up first of all with a coffee in Miss Selfridge and then off she would go, looking in at all the boutiques and bigger stores in and around Oxford Street and Regent Street.

It was also beneficial just to see what the younger people around were wearing. The warmer weather was exposing not just the tops, dresses and skirts girls had on but also gave an insight to the sort of accessories that were popular, something which Joanie hadn't given much consideration to, till now.

It was while she was exploring the cavernous depths of C&A that someone, a girl of similar age to herself, approached.

'Hi. It's Jean, isn't it?'

The voice — only fairly audible above the loud background music — came from someone who she did not immediately recognise. Using her discarded name threw Joanie into a near panic. She frowned, staring back at this stranger.

'It's me, Sue. Sue Parsons. We were at school together.' As Joanie continued to look puzzled, Sue started to feel this must be a case of mistaken identity. 'You are Jean, aren't you? Jean Monckton?'

'Yes. Sorry, I'm afraid I don't remember you.'

'Well, we weren't exactly friends, just in the same class.'

The music seemed to be getting louder, more oppressive. Joanie felt a sort of unreasonable fear that Martin might turn up and wonder who she really was.

The look on her face was beginning to alarm Sue, who was probably wishing she'd never come up and spoken to her.

'You look rather pale, Jean. Why don't I get you outside, into the fresh air?'

Joanie allowed herself to be guided out from the store and back on to the slightly less noisy pavement.

'Why don't we have a coffee, Jean? There's a Wimpy's just along from here. Come on, my treat.'

So it was that Joanie found herself in a Wimpy bar with someone she could hardly remember who only knew her as Jean Monckton. Yet she was touched at the thoughtfulness and compassion this Sue had shown her over her own rather strange behaviour.

'What have you been up to? It seems a lifetime ago since we were at school. Are you married?'

'No,' Joanie said, almost ashamed at the admission. Despite the permissiveness of the Swinging Sixties, a lot of Joanie's former friends had, she knew, gone down the bridal path instead of

27

choosing the road to female liberation. And Sue's slightly conservative appearance suggested she too had chosen the former route.

'How about you?' she asked, mainly out of politeness.

Surprisingly, Sue shook her head.

'No. There was someone but he died.'

It was said in such a matter of fact way that, at first, Joanie wondered if she'd misheard. But no, there was just the slightest trace of moistness appearing in Sue's eyes which she quickly wiped away with a paper napkin. She then leant across towards Joanie.

'You know, I always looked up to you at school. There was something about you — your aloofness or single-mindedness — something. You always struck me as someone who was going to do something with their life — I mean something different from the rest of us. Am I right? Have you?'

Joanie was astonished. The aloofness Sue was referring to was in fact a form of defence. She wasn't particularly popular at school. Her secret acted as a hindrance — an obstacle — in building any meaningful relationships with her peers. Instead she focused on her studies and her ambition to be a fashion designer.

'Well, I do work for myself . . . '

'I knew it!' Sue interrupted, greatly impressed despite not knowing, yet, what that work might entail. 'Let me guess. You're a best-selling author — although wouldn't I have heard of you, if that was the case, unless of course you write under an assumed name. Am I right?'

Well, you are partly right, Joanie thought.

'No,' she said, 'I'm no writer — I'm a fashion designer with my own shop.'

'How exciting,' Sue said, by way of concealing her disappointment. Having more interest in books than clothes, she felt this was not going to be a conversation she would be pursuing for much longer.

Joanie noticed the surreptitious glance at her watch, and began constructing an excuse in her head for leaving. But, just at that moment, a genuine reason appeared. Martin! And then, in the same moment, she saw that it was not possible. How could she approach the man she had no claim on when he was walking along with a rather attractive young woman, who had her arm through his.

'Are you OK, Jean? You've gone almost white. What is it?'

Joanie quickly recovered her composure. It all made sense, suddenly. His hasty telephone call the day before he was due to take a week's holiday; the obviously hollow excuse that he was having to cover for sickness, but was hoping to reschedule as soon as he could. And yet, how could she object? He was not answerable to her as she wasn't to him.

'Jean. You look miles away.'

I wish I were, she thought. I so wish I were.

Baby, Now That I've Found You

Work is the best therapy. The busier you are, the less you have time to dwell on those unpleasant things which are trying to encroach into your life. All well and good, except at night, when all you want to do is fall into a deep, dreamless sleep, but your own thoughts won't allow it. This is how it had become for Joanie. It had been three days — and nights — since she'd seen Martin, with the girl in Oxford Street; three days where she'd kept herself so busy even her Aunt Mary had remarked on it.

'I hope you're not overdoing it, dear. What happened to that holiday you were going to take? I'm sure you need it.'

Joanie shrugged.

'Didn't have time, Auntie. I've had a lot of new orders come in and I can't afford to be late with them.'

This was partly true. Joanie's reputation was beginning to spread and one or two of the bigger names on the high street were showing an interest in carrying some of her ranges in their stores. But, of course, it wasn't the whole truth.

Another week went by, in a bit of a blur. And then, one Tuesday in May, the telephone rang. Joanie was dealing with a customer at the time so let it go on to the answerphone. Even the customer sensed the apparent agitation that Joanie was showing. This kept happening. The phone ringing would set off alarm bells in her own head.

After the customer had left, Joanie quickly headed for the phone to listen to the message. It was, as she feared — hoped — Martin.

'Hi Joanie, sorry I keep missing you. I do actually have a week off starting tomorrow so would very much like to meet up with you again. I find myself thinking about you a lot. Anyway, you've got my number, perhaps you'll give me a call. Bye.'

Joanie sighed. She didn't know whether to be pleased or annoyed by his message. To hear him say he'd been thinking about her a lot only added to her bewilderment.

Again she sighed, deciding reluctantly, as she did so, that it would be better not to respond. It's not to be, she told herself, without any strong feeling of conviction.

★ ★ ★

It was a couple of days later, as Joanie was dealing with a rather pushy salesman, that the shop door opened and Martin stepped in. He was wearing what looked like an expensive Aquascutum jacket over a pale green polo shirt. Instead of trousers to match the jacket, he was wearing his oldest, most favoured faded Levi jeans.

The effect for Joanie was quite distracting and she found she hadn't heard a word the salesman was saying from the moment the door pinged and Martin entered.

At least he hasn't brought flowers, she thought as she finally managed to get rid of the over-zealous salesman.

'Martin,' she said, in a very business-like way, as if he was another salesman.

Martin smiled; that warm, heart-melting smile which distracted — and disturbed — Joanie almost to the point of her losing her resolve not to be taken in by his obvious charm.

'Hello, Joanie. Finally I get to see you.'

'What brings you into this part of town? I would have thought Oxford Street would be more your line of country.'

Martin frowned, genuinely puzzled.

'Oxford Street? I hardly ever go there. As you can see I'm hardly a dedicated follower of fashion.'

'I don't know,' Joanie said, not willing to let Martin get off so lightly, 'I'm sure in the right company you'd look fine.'

Martin's frown deepened.

'You've completely lost me, I'm afraid. I was rather hoping to have you as company — that is, if you can spare the time.'

34

There was an appealing smile spreading from his lips — those attractive lips that had never yet kissed her — which Joanie found impossible to ignore.

'Would you like a coffee? I was just about to put the kettle on.'

'That would be lovely, thank you. But actually the reason I came over was to ask if you'd like to come out to dinner this evening. There's a new Cantonese restaurant in Soho my friends at work keep going on about. I thought it might be nice for the two of us to try it out first hand. What do you say?'

Despite her doubts and misgivings, Joanie found herself agreeing. She hardly ever went out — her business saw to that — or if she did it was usually in some way connected with her work, so it would be nice to be going somewhere purely for her own enjoyment, especially as it was in the company of such a good-looking partner.

★ ★ ★

At seven-thirty that same evening Martin arrived at Mary's house, pulling up in his racing green Austin Healey, the hood down as there was still enough warmth from the day's heat to justify it.

Joanie invited Martin in so that her aunt could meet him. Mary was suitably impressed by this first encounter. Charming was the word that came to mind. She offered them both a drink but their table was booked and waiting.

'Another time perhaps,' Martin politely said.

'I would like that.'

* * *

The restaurant was busy. A lot of people were either trying it out or coming again because the food was so good. A waiter guided them to a table for two over by the wall. He then flourished the menus before leaving to see to the next customers.

'I like it,' Joanie said. 'It has a really groovy atmosphere.'

Martin smiled. Groovy. Yes, groovy was absolutely the right word for it.

They ordered and then shared a bottle of wine. Some sort of Asiatic music was playing softly in the background, adding to the ambience of the place. It was, as Joanie had said, groovy.

Part way through their meal — Joanie let Martin decide for them; her experience of exotic food was more or less restricted to Vesta meals — a man, of more or less similar age to Martin but with an almost sneering expression on his face, stopped to speak as he, and a woman, old enough to be his mother, were going past Martin and Joanie's table on their way out.

'Evening, young Smithy,' he said, stopping and staring at Joanie, the sneer transforming to a leer. Joanie, feeling uncomfortable, glanced up at the man's companion, thinking she might be jealous or annoyed by his behaviour, but she was simply gazing blankly into an unfocused point in the distance, appearing totally indifferent.

The man, having been introduced as Simon something or other, was prattling on; something about a girl. Joanie was only beginning to listen, but as she did, her enjoyment was turning to puzzlement as to what she was hearing.

'How is Paula? Gorgeous as ever, no doubt. I last saw her a month or so ago — with you actually. I called out but you couldn't have heard, all that traffic noise and crowds. I don't know why people want to come to London, I really don't.'

The woman, suddenly awake, gave the man a none too subtle dig in the ribs, as if she were trying to get a reluctant horse to move. What you need is a riding crop, Joanie thought. That might get through his thick skin.

They left but somehow the man's unpleasant presence seemed to linger and it became impossible to recapture the previous intimate pleasure that she and Martin had been enjoying. And, not having yet had a chance to get to know him, Joanie felt she had no right to quiz him on this girl Paula, as much as she wanted to.

★　★　★

As Martin pulled up outside Mary Saunders's house, he switched off the engine and turned to face Joanie.

'I'm sorry the evening didn't turn out quite as we expected. That Simon, he just rubs me up the wrong way. And, of course, I have to listen to him; he's my boss.'

'That's all right. I didn't mind.'

Martin said nothing but continued to look at Joanie. Finally, the words came out.

'You are so beautiful, Joanie. All evening I've just wanted to kiss you.'

And before either of them knew it, they had both, simultaneously, moved closer towards each other till their lips met in a long embrace. And, at once, everything changed for the better.

The Wind Cries Mary

The next week passed in a haze of happiness. Although Joanie couldn't spend every day with Martin she did cut her hours so they could spend as much time as possible together.

On the final day of his break — the Sunday — Martin took Joanie to the coast, to Margate, where they had a wonderful time in the unseasonably warm sunshine, sitting on the beach, swimming in the sea and going on as many rides as possible in Dreamland. Martin even managed to bag Joanie a big, fluffy teddy bear on the firing range.

With every physical moment they were spending together they were getting emotionally close as well. Joanie, for the first time in her life, was feeling herself committed to the prospect of falling in love. And Martin was showing every indication of going the same way, too.

'I'll ring you when I get back from Sydney,' Martin said, as he pulled up outside Aunt Mary's house. The hour was late but it looked, surprisingly, as if Mary was still up.

'I've had a wonderful time,' Joanie said, hugging closely the fluffy teddy bear which would always be a reminder of the culmination of their week together.

'Are you speaking to him or me?' Martin grinned.

Joanie smiled.

'I'm not sure. I don't know who I love more; Teddy or you.'

Although said as a sort of joke, it was nevertheless the first time that the word love had come up in the time they'd spent together.

And Joanie, in that moment, realised that that, indeed, was what she was feeling for Martin, despite concealing her true feelings behind a toy bear.

Martin's expression had also changed. He wore a serious look on his usually cheerful face. He leant across and they kissed, and this time it felt, to Joanie, that Martin was — like her — giving into his own heart's call.

When they'd stopped and sat back again, Martin still had that expression on his face, but there was a softness in the seriousness.

'I do love you, Joanie,' he managed to whisper, after a while.

'I love you, too.'

They embraced again but this time the teddy bear somehow managed to lodge itself between the loving pair. Laughter ensued.

'I'd better go. It looks as if Auntie's been waiting up for me.'

'I'll see you soon, my darling.'

She waited just inside the gate and waved Martin off, feeling her life was changed for ever. Then, still with a smile on her face, she walked up the garden path and let herself in.

'Hello, dear. Did you have a nice time?' Mary didn't sound like her usual, cheerful self. The way she spoke just then sounded mechanical. She was seated in one of the armchairs alongside the fireplace in the front room. Joanie flopped down on the one opposite, and then immediately sat up again.

'Is everything all right, Auntie?'

Mary was looking tired and pre-occupied, and was making no attempt to conceal it.

'I'm not sure, dear.'

Joanie leapt from her chair and went quickly across to her aunt, taking her hand as she knelt down in front of her.

'What is it, Auntie? Are you not well?' Mary, by way of answer gave her niece a tired smile, shaking her head as she did so. 'Then what is it? You must tell me. Has someone upset you?'

There was an indication of tears developing in Mary's eyes.

'I have been upset, yes, but not in the way you think. I saw someone today who I hadn't seen since nineteen forty-one.'

'Really? And what was it about this person that upset you?'

Mary released her hand from Joanie's grip.

'Go and sit down, dear. It can't be comfortable kneeling down.'

Joanie slowly raised herself, resumed

her place in the other chair, and waited for her aunt to explain.

'I met the man I thought I was going to marry.'

Despite the matter of fact way that Mary said it, the effect on Joanie was literally jaw dropping.

'You thought you were going to marry? What happened? Why didn't you?'

As she asked these questions, Joanie reminded herself of what she'd thought previously about her aunt's almost quaint outlook on romance. So there had been someone after all.

'It was the war, dear . . . things were so much different then. People were behaving in ways that they might not otherwise have done.

'I knew several girls who got married to men they barely knew. Others, like myself and Ray, just kept putting it off. He didn't think it would be fair — on me — for us to make a commitment in such unpredictable, dangerous times.'

'Yes, but what happened when the war ended? Why didn't you marry then?'

Mary sighed.

'Because I never saw him again. He was reported missing presumed dead, and eventually I had to accept it as true.'

'But he wasn't. And now he's turned up all these years later. What did he say? What could he say?' Joanie was feeling both indignant and angry on her aunt's behalf. Mary, however, appeared quite calm.

'He was very pleasant, in a sort of awkward way. He said how glad he was to see me, and that he was sorry it had been so long.'

'How did he know where to find you, Auntie?'

'Well, dear, I am still living in the same house as I was back then, remember? As I always had done. It was your grandparents' house originally, and then when your mother gave you up into my care she agreed that I should continue to live here with you.'

How very generous of her, Joanie thought, but managed not to say. Instead, she pursued her line of questioning, feeling a strong sense of protective loyalty towards this good woman who'd put everyone else's needs before her own.

'So, what were his reasons for wanting to see you after all this time?'

Mary explained that Ray, a seasoned pilot in the RAF, had been shot down during a bombing raid over France. He'd managed to free himself from the cockpit and then was able to parachute down to an open field, somewhere in southern France.

He expected to be picked up by the Germans but to his surprise — and relief — it was a local group of resistance fighters who came to his rescue, having seen his parachute illuminated by the flames from his plane as it too descended to earth.

'To cut a long story short,' Mary continued, 'he was sheltered by these people at a farm. The Germans were everywhere so escape became impossible. So he joined their resistance group and stayed with them for the remainder of the war.'

Joanie frowned.

'That still doesn't explain why you've not heard from him, once the war was over, I mean. After all, it's been over twenty years since the war ended . . . '

'He'd got married, to a French girl — one of the resistance people who sheltered him. It was her parents' farm that he lived in.'

'Oh, Auntie, how awful.'

Mary shrugged and tried to smile.

'As I said, the war did strange things to people. He could hardly be blamed for being shot down. And then, I suppose, fate intervened.'

'But what I can't understand is why he should be seeking you out now, just to tell you that he'd met someone else. It almost seems cruel.'

Mary shook her head.

'No, it wasn't cruel. He'd felt guilty at marrying someone else when, presumably, we were together. But, of course, we weren't — neither physically nor emotionally. But I think it had always troubled his conscience that his heart had overruled his head. He'd never told

47

his wife — or anyone — of his circumstances before landing in France.'

'Why, though, has he come back now, to find you and tell you things you maybe wouldn't want to hear?'

'His wife died last year and he somehow felt it gave him the opportunity to put things right between us. Her parents' farm was thriving and with extra people they'd taken on it seemed a good time to come over.'

'And what did you have to say to all this?'

Mary looked distinctly sheepish and would not meet Joanie's eyes.

'I'm afraid I told a lie. I told him I too had married and still was and that my husband would be home soon and might not be too happy to find a former boyfriend on his doorstep.'

Joanie clapped her hands.

'Good for you, Auntie! So, did he go?'

'Yes, but not before saying that he was staying on in London for a few more days and that, should I want to get in touch, he gave me the telephone number of the hotel where he was staying.'

'The cheek of him!'

Mary frowned.

'Not really, dear. He was — is — a good man; a good man with a troubled conscience. I think I may have acted a little too hastily, sending him off like that.'

'Sounds as if you're well rid of him, Auntie.'

'Don't say that, Joanie. I only have happy memories of my time with him, and I won't let anything spoil that.'

'I'm sorry, Auntie. It's none of my business, really. I just don't want to see you hurt.'

'I won't be,' Mary said. And, as Joanie went up to her room, she wondered exactly what her aunt meant by that last remark.

The Letter

Joanie still had concerns for her aunt's welfare the next morning but decided not to say any more on the subject. Although it was Monday and, in theory, she did not have to go to the shop today, she nevertheless did, wanting some structure and normality back in her life.

It had been a rollercoaster of a week both literally and emotionally, and her aunt's revelation had added to the mix. She needed the calm, focused concentration of her work to settle her down, in some ways, back to earth.

She had some hand sewing to do on some tops she'd made where she was adding a few appliqués to embellish the designs. She decided against the CND emblem and opted, instead, for butterflies.

As much as she was in favour of banning the bomb, she didn't want her fashions sending out her own political views. Besides, butterflies, in their own way, epitomised peace, in all its manifestations.

By about mid morning her back and eyes were beginning to feel the strain so she decided to get an espresso at the nearby milk bar. The owner, Tony, called it an emporium and was justly proud of its appearance and reputation.

It was a survivor of the Fifties and, who knew, one day — if it continued — it might well enjoy the status of a listed building. It was a chrome and glass and tiled marvel; all those surfaces highly polished and gleaming, and the coffee and sandwiches totally mouthwatering.

She came from the back room and was heading towards the front door when she noticed a young woman peering in at the window.

Joanie couldn't be sure if the person in question was admiring the display — trouser suits and hats and bags — or whether she was trying to see further into the shop itself. She had her hand cupped over her eyes, its shadow concealing the rest of her face somewhat.

And yet, there was something disturbingly familiar about her, although Joanie couldn't think why.

'Hello,' she said, opening the door. 'Would you like to come in and have a look round?'

The girl was about her own age, and looked guardedly back, like a wild animal sensing a trap.

'It says you're closed today.'

'It is, yes, and I'm not usually here but, as I am, you're welcome to come in.'

The young woman stared back at Joanie for quite a while, as if to memorise her features. Finally, she spoke.

'No, I don't think so, thank you. I was just passing.' And then she swept away without a backward glance.

For the rest of the day the young woman's face seemed to haunt Joanie. She felt certain she'd seen her before. Could it have been at any one of the fashion shows she had attended, or maybe at someone's party?

She could be a journalist for one of the many magazines which proliferated the industry, but none of these possibilities, for some reason, seemed likely.

Her clothes alone had suggested to Joanie that she would more likely be going to M&S rather than C&A. So, what would bring her to A La Mod on a Monday morning, not the obvious day for clothes shopping, the reason why Joanie very seldom opened on that day. It was a mystery and, for some reason, it troubled her.

By around midday Joanie decided to go back home. As well as the image of the young woman who'd appeared at Joanie's shop, she was also still concerned by her aunt's encounter with the man whom she had intended to marry, and the effect it had had on her.

Mary was in when Joanie arrived home and had been preparing lunch for herself.

'I'm making a sandwich, dear. Would you like one?'

'If it's no trouble, Auntie.'

'No trouble at all.'

Joanie sat down at the kitchen table,

discreetly scrutinising her aunt for any tell tale signs of . . . what? She couldn't say. Nor did she feel she could bring up the subject herself. In some ways it was none of her business. It was just that she didn't want her aunt getting hurt by meeting this man, Roy — no, Ray.

The second post arrived. Joanie went to pick up the mail on the hall doormat. It comprised just the one item, and it was addressed to herself.

'What was it?' Mary casually asked, as Joanie returned to the kitchen.

'I don't know. It looks rather official.' She then noticed the franking. 'It's local.'

'Well, aren't you going to open it?' Mary said, placing a plate with a cheese and pickle sandwich on the table.

Joanie did open it. What it contained was a printed wedding invitation. Joanie read it out.

'You are cordially invited to the wedding taking place at Hillford Register Office between Mrs Celia Margaret Monckton and Mr Henry Albert Smythe on Friday August 4th 1967 at 4 o'clock.

RSVP.'

Underneath, hastily written in Mrs Monckton's own hand, were the words: 'Obviously this applies to you both.'

'It's for both of us,' Joanie said unconvincingly.

Mary raised an eyebrow.

'I expect it is. Now, come along, eat your sandwich.'

★ ★ ★

A few days later, Joanie received a postcard from Martin, from Sydney, Australia; a photo of Bondi beach on the front. The message it contained was somewhat restrained, allowing for the postman reading it as well as Joanie.

But he did say he missed her and was looking forward to seeing her soon. Despite its lack of feeling — or ardour, as she imagined, not unkindly, that her aunt would use to describe it — Joanie felt both comforted and reassured by his thoughtfulness. Halfway round the world and he still thinks of me.

Now that they had both declared their love for one another, Joanie had rebuilt her trust in Martin. There was no doubt a perfectly simple explanation for him to have been out with a girl in Oxford Street.

But she wasn't going to ask him for it; she felt that that might be asking for trouble, and she didn't want any more of that in her life.

You Keep Me Hanging On

When Martin next returned there was never enough time to meet. Joanie, as she'd hoped and expected, had been asked to submit a sample range to one of the big names in the high street, and producing enough items to show them was not only very time consuming but it also seemed to be constantly on her mind.

Martin, although enthusiastic and supportive, had no real idea of just what was involved.

Also the summer holiday season was getting well under way and he was finding himself having to take on extra flights to help meet the ever-growing demands of the new wave of foreign holiday enthusiasts.

As he made yet another cup of coffee in the back room of Joanie's shop, and as the clock ticked on past any chance of going anywhere, he recollected — almost nostalgically — that Dreamland and

Margate seemed a lifetime away.

July was, mostly for Joanie, spent this way. She was well aware that she was not giving Martin the time he deserved but this was an opportunity too good to pass up. She understood clearly that when you run your own business its needs, almost invariably, come first.

But at least Martin could get away, even if it was as part of his job. The variety of destinations must be constantly stimulating, unlike how it currently was for Joanie, in the same place, in almost always the same position, with the prospect of nothing more than going back home, having something to eat and heading for bed where, as soon her head hit the pillow, she would be asleep.

She would have loved a holiday, however brief, something that she and Martin could share, just the two of them. But it wouldn't be happening any time soon.

And then there was her mother's wedding to get through.

She hadn't mentioned it to Martin. She hadn't, in fact, told him anything much about her family, her past. Not that he'd asked. That was one of the things which she loved about Martin, that he took her on face value, that he loved her for herself.

Not that she, either, had asked him about his family. She understood that his parents were divorced but that was about it.

'I'm flying out to the Maldives tomorrow,' Martin told her, as he brought the freshly brewed cups to Joanie's work table. 'And then I've got to do Rio. I'm not quite sure, yet, when I'll next be getting time off, back in the UK, I mean.'

Joanie looked up into his lovely blue eyes, which reminded her of their first meeting. They weren't sparkling now, they just looked tired. Tired of me, she couldn't help thinking.

Who wouldn't rather be in Rio, given the choice between a cramped, crowded workroom and a sunny, exotic location. No contest.

★ ★ ★

A week later Joanie was making her first presentation at Passion for Fashion in Carnaby Street. She had been surprised that the shop was not much bigger than her own, and was now having second thoughts about having hired a model to show off her range.

She also felt very nervous and very alone. But the shop's manager and buyer, Anthony, was very warm in his welcome, making Joanie start to feel more relaxed and, importantly, confident.

The model, Susie, did a great job presenting the outfits, making Joanie feel justified in her decision. It also freed her up to talk about each design as they were paraded. Anthony was impressed.

'It has a freshness about it. You remind me of Quant with your originality and enthusiasm. I love it.'

Then came the caveat.

'I can only sample a few items, and, actually, I would really be thinking more about an autumn and winter collection. But I do think it's wonderful what you've done. I love it.'

Joanie thanked him and, after taking what actually was quite a small order, she left the boutique a lot less enthusiastic than when she'd arrived.

'Hey, it was good — you did well.' Susie gave Joanie an affectionate hug before they parted company, but it was little comfort.

Oh, Martin, I wish you were here.

Then, as it started to rain, she changed her mind and wished she were there.

Sittin' in the Park

Mary Saunders, knowing full well that Joanie would be out all day, caught a bus to take her into town for the pre-arranged meeting. She felt almost ashamed at her own subterfuge but Joanie had enough on her mind without her aunt adding to her concerns.

But why should it be of any concern, she told herself. I'm simply meeting up with an old friend I haven't seen in over 20 years.

But, of course, it wasn't as simple as that — nothing ever is, as both she and Joanie knew only too well. But she had made up her mind. She shouldn't have lied to Ray; it wasn't right.

'Tell the truth and shame the devil,' her mother used to say and Mary had always carried with her, until Ray had appeared on her doorstep.

It took two bus rides to get Mary anywhere near the hotel Ray was staying at. It was set modestly back in a quiet suburban avenue some distance from the centre of the capital but, importantly, it gave the hotel a London address.

Two pots of geraniums stood either side of the entrance, their bright red blooms giving a cheery, if misleading, appearance to the exterior of the place at least. Inside, there was a small reception desk where a middle-aged woman, wearing what was probably a permanently fixed harassed look on her face, glanced up as Mary approached, her expression not altering in any way.

'Can I help you?' she said, in a tone of voice that suggested that that was the last thing that she had in mind.

'Is Mr Ray Chambers in?' Polite as Mary usually was, she found herself deliberately not adding 'please' to her question; the receptionist's attitude had aggravated her into doing it.

Besides, now she was here she was starting to feel extremely nervous, and for some reason, by being offhand she hoped it would prevent a breach of her current, concealed, vulnerable emotions.

'Who's asking?' the woman said, persisting in her unsociable manner. But, at that moment, it no longer mattered, as Ray appeared in the lobby and hurried over to the desk.

'Mary! I'm so glad you could come. Here, let me take you through to the restaurant.'

Ray took Mary's arm and gently guided her along the corridor, past the stairs, and into the entrance of the hotel's restaurant.

Its décor, for some reason, gave Mary the impression of being underwater, despite the fact that they were nowhere near the Thames. There was an insipid greeny-blueness which seemed to saturate the room, its gloominess accentuated by the dim lighting and heavy curtains.

Ray noticed Mary's look of distaste as they both stood in the doorway.

'What say we get a cab up to town?' he offered.

'I think that would be a good idea.'

The sun was out, it was warm, and the nearer the taxi took them to the heart of the capital the busier — livelier — it got.

Mary felt inspired, alive. As the taxi started to skirt the Victoria memorial and begin heading down the Mall, she touched Ray's arm.

'Can we stop? I think I'd like to go over there.' She pointed across the road to St James's Park which looked like an oasis of tranquillity in this bustling metropolis.

'Of course.' Ray told the cabbie who very obligingly did a U-turn and dropped them off next to one of the entrances into the park.

'Look, there's a coffee stall. Would you like one?'

'I would, thank you.'

'OK. But wait . . . ' He stopped. 'What about lunch?'

'Actually, I don't think I could manage anything. They do sell sandwiches here, though — if you're hungry, that is.'

'No, I'm not. Coffee would be fine.'

They sat down to drink their coffee on one of the nearby benches. The sun continued shining in a clear blue sky. It

65

really was a perfect summer's day.

'Did you tell your husband you were coming to see me?' Ray said, after a while.

Mary found she could not look him in the face when asked this.

'There was no need,' she eventually said, which was true enough. She needed time to see whether or not it would be necessary to tell him the truth.

'You know, you haven't changed a bit,' Ray said, smiling as he continued to look at Mary.

'Neither have you,' she said, trying to be as tactfully dishonest and chivalrous as he was. For, obviously, they had both changed, not only in their physical appearance which the years had imposed, but in so many other ways, too.

Ray's decision to remain in France, to marry a French girl, never to have told her of what had become of him so that she might have been released, emotionally, from the ache in her heart that had remained with her even, to some extent, to this day . . . some might say his actions were unforgivable.

But Mary was not of that nature. Despite everything, and after the initial shock, she was actually pleased to see Ray. She had loved him then and, in a way, her love had never totally faded.

'What are you thinking?' Ray asked, after they had both been silent for a while.

Mary grinned.

'I was thinking I would love to feed the birds. They're so tame here, they feed right out of your hand.'

Ray bought some sandwiches at the coffee stall and, together, they set off further into the park, closer to the water's edge. A pair of pelicans, seeing Mary unwrap one of the sandwich packs, zoomed in on them, and, for a few minutes, all parties were engrossed in the activity.

'Shall we grab that bench, Mary?'

Mary looked past the bench, towards a spreading plane tree which offered shade against the ever climbing sun.

'Let's go over there, under that tree.

Yes?'

'Certainly.'

Under the tree's canopy there was relief from the increasing heat. It offered, also, a broader view of the park and its visitors.

Mary sighed — a sigh of pleasure.

'I haven't done this in years,' she told Ray. 'I don't suppose you remember. I called it people watching.' She paused to recollect.

'People watching. It's something I've always enjoyed. You see little acts being played out amongst those you take notice of, and then you try to imagine the story behind the actions. It's like having a continuous theatre company working solely on your behalf.'

'I remember.' Ray smiled.

'Do you?' Mary was surprised.

'Yes. I don't know if it was here or some other place but you used to tell me what you thought was going on between a couple, say, or a family with children. It was interesting and amusing.'

'Still, I'm surprised you remember.'

'I remember a lot, Mary.'

They fell silent for a while. Then Ray pointed to a couple who appeared to have met by chance in the open park. The boy and girl stood facing each other, apparently with some sort of issue between them, judging by their stance and body language.

'What's the story there?'

Mary watched in silence before speaking.

'They're breaking up.'

'You can see that?' Ray was impressed.

'Yes. The boy doesn't want to — he wants things to be as they were. But she's telling him things have changed, that they can't go back to how it was. He says he's sorry for not telling her about the things he'd done, and why he wasn't able to marry her until now. But she's saying it's too late for that; her heart still loves him but only as a memory of love.'

As if the girl had been following Mary's narrative, which both she and Mary seemed aware had reached its conclusion, she now turned and walked away from the boy, who remained motionless, eyes fixed on the vanishing figure. Mary quickly stood up.

'The end,' she said brightly, brushing away a few crumbs from her skirt. Ray, less speedily, also stood up and they faced each other in much the same way as the young couple they'd been watching had stood.

Ray reached out tentatively to take Mary's hand which she allowed.

'It needn't be the end,' he said.

Mary nodded.

'No, it needn't be, but we must look at it as a new — a different — beginning.'

'I know I was wrong not to tell you what had happened to me. And how I felt about Francoise was so completely different to how I felt — feel — about you. I owed Francoise my life . . .'

Mary squeezed Ray's hand.

'Let's not talk about it any more. What's done is done. The past is over, like the war. I'm really glad you came to see me and I want to remain friends.'

'What about your husband? Do you think he'll mind?'

Mary smiled.

'There is no husband — never was. I just needed a sort of barrier, to protect me when you turned up out of the blue.'

Ray frowned.

'So, did you never marry?'

Mary shook her head.

'I am so sorry. I feel I've ruined your life.'

'Don't be silly, Ray. I've had — and am still having — a good life. Your turning up obviously had an effect on me, but now I'm getting used to it. I'm really glad you found me. I'm just sorry it had to be as a result of your family's tragedy.'

They talked a little more, finding it helped to ease their manner towards one another. Then it was time to head back home — for Mary, at least.

'You're not catching any bus,' Ray insisted, hailing a taxi. On the journey back, Ray continued to hold Mary's hand. It felt comfortable, natural to them both, and it furthered Mary's resolve to ask him something which had been on her mind for a good part of the day.

Standing in the Shadows of Love

Martin, yawning, sat on the edge of his sofa bed staring at the card he held in his hand. The journey back from Rio had left him feeling tired and drained. He'd even left his car at the airport and got a taxi back to his flat in Richmond.

He had been intending to have a quick bath and then some sleep before phoning Joanie. He was aware that their relationship had stalled, due, he acknowledged, to her work, but, nevertheless, it had made him feel as if he were becoming surplus to requirements.

And now this. As he re-read the card his mind was in a turmoil. What would they think? Would he go? Finally, unable to answer his own recurring questions, he dropped the card on the floor and let himself fall back on to the sofa bed where he promptly fell asleep for nearly four hours.

When he awoke it had already started to get dark which gave him a feeling of lonely isolation. He tried to shrug it off, thinking he must have dreamed something to make him feel this low. A bath would put him right, help him snap out of this negative mood.

And then he sat up and saw the card which he'd dropped on the floor four hours earlier. He stooped to pick it up, hoping he might have misread it, or that this was the dream and that when he awoke everything would be OK again. But, of course, it wasn't, and the words remained the same.

★ ★ ★

'How was your day, Auntie?' Joanie asked, as she tucked into the coronation chicken which Mary had made specially for her, knowing how it had always been Joanie's favourite.

'It was good, dear. We went to St James's park.'

Joanie stopped eating and looked

74

across pointedly at her aunt.

'We?'

Joanie didn't put another forkful in her mouth until Mary had given her a full account of what she had been doing that day, and of the question which Mary had finally put to Ray once the taxi had eventually pulled up outside her house.

'And what did he say?' Joanie asked, trying her best to conceal her misgivings.

'He said yes.' Mary looked very pleased, which Joanie struggled to get her head round.

But there was obviously no point in putting across any of her concerns. She would have to accept that her aunt should know better than she did what she was doing. And, apart from anything else, it did seem to have put a sparkle in her eyes.

Later, lying on her bed — it was another humid night which having a window open did nothing to alleviate — Joanie wondered whether Martin was back from . . . Rio?

The fact that she wasn't sure which

destination he was returning from signalled the distance, emotionally, that seemed to be growing between them — never mind the air miles. Should she contact him or should she just wait to hear?

This bewildering dilemma brought to mind her aunt's situation and it only added fuel to her own apparent predicament. Only I'm not going to wait 20 years for an answer, she told herself before finally falling asleep.

I'll Never Fall in Love Again

As it happened, Joanie only had to wait till later the following day when Martin telephoned the shop. She hastily turned off the transistor radio, despite it playing her favourite song, 'All You Need Is Love'.

'A La Mod, hello.'

'Hello, Joanie. It's Martin.'

'Hello, Martin.' Joanie was sounding as guarded as he was. She noted, ironically, that the summer of love was no longer having the same impact on her that so many other young people were experiencing. And she couldn't really explain or understand why.

Perhaps they had rushed their relationship, although she didn't think they had. Perhaps Martin was gradually losing interest, although, if that was the case, why keep contacting her?

'Are you still there?'

What neither of them realised was that they were both preoccupied with the same thing, which had nothing and everything to do with them, both individually and together.

'Yes. How was Brazil?'

'Hot, very hot. And it was Rio, actually. A bit too crowded for my liking. How have you been getting on? Did you get that order you were going for?'

'Not exactly.' Joanie was reluctant to explain to Martin the terms of the deal Passion for Fashion had struck with her — not because it was top secret or anything like that but because she felt guilty at all that lost time that she and Martin could have better spent being together and enjoying themselves.

'Didn't they like your stuff? They'd be mad not to.'

Joanie allowed herself a smile at Martin's reaction to her disappointing news. After all, he was hardly a fashion guru. It would be a bit like that girl who'd been peering in at her window the other week saying something similar.

And just as she thought this she felt her heart freeze almost. That girl! Of course! It was her! She was the one on Martin's arm that day in Oxford Street. That's why she seemed so familiar.

So, she thought she'd come and see for herself who this other girl was who Martin had been paying attention to. But even as she thought it she could see it didn't make sense.

How could she have known about Joanie unless Martin had told her, which he would have been very unlikely to do? And yet, he must have done. Why else would she turn up, without any intention of buying anything, if not to check out the competition, as it were?

'Hello? Joanie? You've gone again. Can you hear me?'

'I have to go. I've got a customer. Bye.'

She put the phone down, not giving Martin a chance to ask her out — if that was what his purpose had been. I won't be strung along, she told herself. My name's not Mary Saunders.

As soon as Joanie arrived home that evening Mary told her that Martin had phoned.

'He seemed a bit concerned, dear. Have you had a falling out?'

'No, we haven't,' Joanie replied impatiently. 'Look, I just need to freshen up, Auntie. It's been a long day and I'm feeling whacked.'

'Of course. I'll go and see to the dinner. Would you like a glass of something to go with it? I bought a rather nice Riesling today. I thought we could share some.'

'I'm not really hungry, Auntie, but I will have a glass of wine, thank you.'

After a long, soothing Radox bath, Joanie felt a whole lot better. She had decided to adopt a laissez faire attitude because, actually, her life was full enough without any emotional entanglements right now.

It was probably impossible to combine a happy and successful love/life/work existence, and as the only certain thing in her life was her business it was probably best to stick with that and make the best of it as she possibly could.

'This Riesling's rather nice, Auntie,' Joanie commented, as they sat opposite one another in the two old armchairs by the fireplace.

'We should drink a toast,' Mary said, raising her glass. 'To absent friends.'

Mary, having never been much of a drinker, was seemingly a little light-headed after having drunk two glasses. This might have explained her some-what inappropriate toast.

'Who are they, Auntie?'

Mary shrugged, her glass still raised.

'Oh, I don't know. I guess there's always someone absent though, don't you?'

'Cheers,' Joanie said.

Friday on My Mind

It was August already. And in just three days from now Joanie's mother would be getting married. Joanie had still not made up her mind whether or not to attend.

'You decide for yourself, dear. It's up to you.'

'It just seems . . . I don't know.'

'Weird?' Mary offered, recalling Joanie's use of the word before, regarding her mother's initial announcement of her forthcoming marriage.

'Yes, probably. Will you be going?'

'I think so. I have no reason not to. And I'm rather interested in seeing her husband to be.'

Joanie smiled. Really, Aunt Mary was an incurable romantic.

★ ★ ★

At A La Mod, Joanie was putting the finishing touches to designs which Anthony at Passion for Fashion had opted to buy. Not many but it's a start, she told herself. No-one ever made it big overnight, not even Mary Quant. However, this begged the question as to just how big Joanie wanted to be.

She liked her shop and the steady wave of customers it brought — many of them returning customers — but she couldn't see herself wanting more than this. There were already enough big fish in this comparatively small pond of the fashion world. Look at Zandra Rhodes. She, deservedly, led the vanguard of the best of British designers and Joanie was happy enough to be swimming along in her wake.

Besides, life wasn't all about work, although without her work she might find she had too much time in which to dwell on her love life or lack of it.

★ ★ ★

Martin felt that part of his problems had been solved, simply by the fact that he would be flying out to Lisbon on the third and would not be back till some time later the following day.

At least it would be one thing less to concern himself with, and that he could justifiably be exonerated from any blame or criticism.

But that still did not answer the questions buzzing around his head regarding Joanie. He didn't know where he stood any more with her. She was the most desirable and yet infuriating woman he had ever known.

And since she abruptly finished their brief and stilted conversation on the phone the other day, he was nervous and hesitant about contacting her again.

Perhaps she saw him as just a brief diversion in her busy and obviously preferred way of life. Perhaps; perhaps not. How would he ever know?

* * *

August the fourth. It was the morning of Joanie's mother's wedding; a warm, dry sunny day in prospect, so that, at least, was good. But still Joanie remained undecided as to whether or not she would be going. It would mean shutting up shop early, even if only a couple of hours. A couple of hours on a Friday afternoon, though not as busy as a Saturday, might still mean a significant loss to her income.

The wedding was set for four o'clock, so, in some ways, it still gave her a few hours' grace in order to make up her mind one way or the other.

Not so Mary Saunders. She had risen early and was heading off for a nine-thirty appointment at the hairdresser's. Joanie wondered if she might not have been so enthusiastic, or so concerned about her appearance were it not for her 'plus one'. Ray would be coming over and having lunch, and then he was going to change into his suit before they both set off for the wedding.

Had Joanie been there to witness the two of them heading out, she would have been excused for thinking that it was in fact they who were going off to get married instead of simply being the guests at Mary's sister's wedding.

Joanie, however, soon found herself engrossed in her work, driving all thoughts of the significant event taking place later in the day from her mind.

The shop had a steady stream of customers all morning, easing off a little by lunchtime, allowing Joanie a brief respite to pop out and buy a sandwich. Whilst waiting for the kettle to boil in the back room, Joanie now did find her thoughts straying from her work to her mother's wedding day.

In normal circumstances this would be a day for all family members to celebrate. There would be much interaction between parent and children and any other relatives, lots of things to go through, to discuss, to order, and so on and so on. But nothing like that was happening or, even after the actual ceremony, was likely to.

They should have got married in one of those Elvis chapels in Vegas, Joanie thought, trying to stem an almost

uncontrollable feeling of bitter-
ness — and loneliness — that she was
feeling, thinking about it all. It's a farce,
and I'm not going.

★ ★ ★

It was getting close to four o'clock when
Joanie jumped off the bus in Hillford
town centre.

The day had remained warm and
sunny, the only bright spot in it as far as
Joanie was concerned. She still couldn't
quite believe how she could have
persuaded herself to come. Guilt? Conscience?

She couldn't say. But here she was,
with just a few minutes in hand before her
mother's wedding was taking place, setting off, in determined fashion, towards
the town's register office.

She'd even changed for the event, putting on one of her newly designed, flower
patterned trouser suits with a Fedora hat
in a shade of green which complemented
the colours on her clothing.

Why am I doing this? she asked herself again. It was not, she felt, as if her mother would care. Why change the habits of a lifetime? But it was a lifelong burden she carried, trying — without ever succeeding — to please her mother and somehow win back that elusive love which Celia Monckton had always withheld.

As she walked up the steps which led to the entrance to the register office she could feel her heart racing.

As she opened the heavy, oak-panelled door leading into the building she sighed. This is not what it should be like, she was thinking, as she stepped silently across the plush carpeted hallway. Anticipation, excitement, yes. Not fear, or dread.

Opening the door as quietly as she could into the actual wedding venue, she could see the few people who were already in attendance, including Aunt Mary and her friend, Ray.

Mary turned and smiled sweetly at Joanie, indicating a place for her next to them. Celia Monckton — soon to be Smythe — also turned. She smiled, too, but it never extended to her eyes. And then the registrar appeared and the service began.

★ ★ ★

Martin, too, had been struggling with his conscience. His flight back from Lisbon had landed early due to a following wind. Back at his flat the first thing he did was phone Joanie. She had been constantly on his mind and he wanted to show her, in the time honoured way, how much he loved her.

He felt again in his blazer pocket for the reassuring shape of the small square box which contained the ring he had bought at the little jeweller's in Lisbon.

He hoped he wouldn't frighten her off by making this declaration so early on in his relationship with Joanie. It was just that he'd never felt like this before. There had been other girls but not once did he feel with any of them what he felt for Joanie.

These thoughts, hopes, fears, were going round his head all the while the phone rang, firstly at her shop and then at her aunt's. No reply in either case, reminding him, nervously, of that Beatles song of the same name which did not end happily.

Having realised he was not going to be able to speak to Joanie he considered his next option, pondering whether to go or not, and then, if so, what the most appropriate outfit would be.

As he had said to Joanie, he was not exactly a dedicated follower of fashion which was proved beyond any reasonable doubt once he'd opened his wardrobe doors. The suit it would have to be.

He glanced at his watch. If the traffic wasn't too heavy he might just make it in time.

The wedding ceremony was over. There was a photographer from the local paper waiting outside for the arrival of the happy couple. 'The Hillford Gazette' always did this, there was nothing unusual about it. It was a free service where they published the photos in their Tuesday edition guaranteeing extra sales.

'A bit more of a smile, maybe, Mrs?' the somewhat over-familiar young photographer suggested. This, however, had the reverse effect, leaving the sub-editor on the Monday night not sure whether to include it with all the other obviously happy newly-weds.

There was to be a modest, short reception back at Celia's house. She and her new husband, Henry, got into the waiting taxi and sped away, leaving the small scattering of remaining guests seemingly stranded on the pavement.

'My car's just round the corner,' Ray told Joanie. 'I hope you'll come with us.'

Joanie could see no justification in refusing. Ray — on the surface, at least — seemed a very pleasant guy. A gentleman, as Aunt Mary might say.

At the house there was a modest spread — some petit fours, canapes, even a cake. Four bottles of Asti Spumante completed the picture. A depressing sight, Joanie couldn't help thinking. People started to arrive, including neighbours and soon the atmosphere started to warm up a little.

Henry more than made up for his bride's apparent indifference to the whole business, begging the question, why bother getting married at all?

Ray was a most considerate host to his own little circle of Mary and Joanie, refilling their glasses and supplying canapes. As he took back their empty glasses, Mary turned to her niece.

'What did your mother say when you went up to congratulate her?'

'Thank you.' Joanie's expression was unreadable as she said this.

'Nothing else?'

'Nothing else. Oh,' she suddenly remembered, 'she did let me kiss her.'

On Ray's return, Mary suggested they might leave.

'Do you want to come with us, Joanie?'

'Oh, yes, please,' Joanie said, possibly a little over-enthusiastically.

They made their excuses. Henry was

disappointed but Celia didn't seem to mind one way or the other.

Halfway down the road, heading towards Ray's car, Joanie realised she'd left her hat.

'Won't be a minute,' she called out as she dashed back to the house.

She'd retrieved her hat and was making her way along the hall when the doorbell rang. Henry, in the kitchen, called out to Joanie to answer it, which she did, and found herself face to face with Martin. Before either of them could speak, Henry's voice boomed out again.

'Who is it, Jean?'

'Jean?' Martin repeated, a deep frown etching his brow. By now Henry had arrived at the door himself. 'Martin! So glad you could make it.' He then turned to Joanie. 'This is my son, Jean. Jean, meet Martin.'

'We've already met,' Joanie said, her head spinning.

'No, we haven't,' Martin said angrily, brushing past both the dumbfounded Joanie and the equally astonished Henry.

At the end of the hall, unsure where to go next or whether, indeed, he should be here at all, he turned to have one final snipe at Joanie. 'I don't know you.'

Joanie, angry, humiliated, ran from the house, putting as much distance between herself and the humiliation as she possibly could. How could life be so cruel? It seemed that, at every turn, she was destined to be hurt, to never know love — true love — and happiness, unconditional happiness.

What Becomes of the Broken-Hearted?

Well, as far as Joanie was concerned, she'd had a lucky escape. The whole situation was absurd, farcical. But how was she to know? What kind of cruel fate had set her up to fail with Martin? To allow her, first, to fall in love with him and then knock her down hard by telling her she'd given her heart to her stepbrother! It didn't bear thinking about, and Joanie was not going to think about it. The only reminder would be the ache in her heart which, she hoped, would ease with time.

Mary — and Ray — were both unaware of these circumstances, so Joanie decided to keep them ignorant of the true facts. There was no need for anyone to know what a fool she'd been — and what a fool Martin had made of her.

It was those cruel words he'd said at her mother's house that she still couldn't erase from her memory, the last words he would ever say to her, and they hurt, like arrows, piercing her vulnerability.

Work was the only answer. Fortunately, Anthony at Passion for Fashion had come back with a repeat order on a couple of Joanie's designs but, as is the case with the fashion industry, they wanted a quick turnaround. The fashion world is so fickle — as are the people who purchase the goods — and trends can change almost overnight, so Joanie needed to stay focused on getting the goods to Anthony on time, if not before!

'I love your professionalism, Joanie,' Anthony said, as she delivered the ordered outfits. 'And I love your designs — such a bold use of colours, and they all work.'

Joanie felt herself blushing with all the compliments, although she knew well enough just how professional she was. She took a pride in her work. Her designs were a reflection on herself, on both her ability and understanding of what young people wanted.

'Usual thirty day terms, OK?' Anthony called out over his shoulder as he took the outfits through to the storeroom.

'Yes, of course.' Joanie smiled. 'That's fine.'

He came back out from the storeroom, looking at his watch.

'I'm just about to close, actually, so do you fancy going for a drink?'

'That would be nice, thank you.' For some reason, the offer of a drink pleased Joanie. It was, she supposed, because since the Martin débâcle she had not been given any real boost to her confidence till now, where a good-looking young man wanted to take her — Joanie — out for a drink.

She hoped she wasn't reading too much into this simple offer. It was just pleasant for someone to be smiling at her without — as in Aunt Mary's case — it being out of sympathy rather than open friendliness.

They were spoilt for choice for places to drink but Anthony, as it happened, had one particular venue in mind: the Cockney Pride in Piccadilly.

'You don't mind if we walk, do you?'

Anthony asked, as he was locking up the shop.

'Not at all, it's a lovely evening.'

It was. The humidity was gone and, despite being in the heart of the capital, it seemed very pleasant to be on these famous, well worn pavements in the sloping rays of the August sun.

'Tell me about yourself, Joanie,' Anthony suggested, as they walked.

Joanie wasn't going to fall into the trap of 'There's nothing much to say' but she would be careful in not overstating her talents, at the same time keeping her own personal details to herself.

'It's a tough business,' Anthony acknowledged, as they approached the pub, 'but I can't imagine doing anything else.'

'Me neither.'

The place was busy.

'You find a table while I get us drinks,' Anthony said. Joanie looked all around. Just then a couple got up from a table by the door so Joanie quickly moved in.

'There you go, Joanie. Cheers.'

'Cheers.' She raised her vodka and bitter lemon to Anthony's pint of Red Barrel. He then took a surprisingly long, deep swig from his glass, draining nearly half of it in one go.

'That's better,' he said. 'I needed that.' He lowered his glass slowly to the table, then looked directly across to Joanie. 'You know, you could be a model. I'd rather have seen you in those outfits you first brought to my shop than that model girl you hired.'

'Susie? I thought she was very good.'

Anthony held up a hand.

'Oh, she was, she was. Don't get me wrong. I just reckon they would have looked better on you.'

Joanie didn't much care for this line of conversation where, somehow, the emphasis was on her body, she imagined, rather than her clothes. She tried changing the subject.

'Do you have anything in mind for your autumn and winter range?'

'All bought, actually. We may have some gaps in those ranges which you might well help to fill but otherwise all sewn up.'

Anthony looked around the bar as he lifted the pint glass to his lips. Joanie sipped at her drink, wishing she could knock it back in one go and then get out of here.

You really can't mix business with pleasure, she realised, watching Anthony tilting his glass right back to drain its contents.

Also, she was finding herself unconsciously comparing Anthony's behaviour to Martin's and, despite her changed feelings towards the latter, she found herself wishing that in this place, right now, she could be sitting opposite him instead of Anthony. But that was never going to happen.

There's a Kind of Hush

Celia, the new Mrs Smythe, had gone with her husband to the South of France for their honeymoon.

Mary had gone, with Ray, to Lepe in Hampshire to see the places where some of the troops involved in the Normandy landings were stationed before setting off on that momentous June day in 1944, many of whom never to return.

Ray would show where the Mulberry harbours had been anchored in readiness. There were still signs of where they had been, along with gun batteries along this stretch of coastline.

And Martin? Where was he? And how was it that he and his father's surname differed as they did? But then, as Joanie grudgingly reminded herself, she was in no position to pass judgement. No, it was no good dwelling on all the if-onlys and maybes that knowing him had brought up now.

They had been happy in their

ignorance, blissfully, blindly happy, and they could have gone on like that if her own mother hadn't — for whatever reason — agreed to get married again.

Nothing could ever be the same again, it would be ridiculous. So there was nothing for it but to get back into concentrating on her work, on producing some new innovative lines, but it seemed that all her energy, concentration and imagination had dissipated, leaving her with an emptiness that, currently, both her heart and her home was exposing her to.

Mary had said she would be away for just a few days before Ray was going to have to return to France to take up the reins again, running the farm.

Joanie knew she was being selfish begrudging her aunt these few moments of happiness in what had been, after all, an unfulfilled life. It was just that she hated waking up to an empty house almost as much as she hated coming home to an empty one.

August, what remained of it, was

always a dead month. Factories closed for their annual summer holidays which meant that nothing very much was going on in the commercial world.

Joanie had decided against producing any more designs for Passion for Fashion, especially as it looked as though Anthony was not actually selling her clothes in his shop but was unstitching them and having patterns made up before shipping them across to Hong Kong to have them produced at a fraction of what it would cost in the UK. Joanie knew but somehow lacked the means or the energy to do anything about it. Just be true to yourself, then you can't be let down.

★ ★ ★

Mary's return lifted Joanie's spirits and she made a big fuss of her on that first evening together, even to cooking their dinner, complete with a bottle of Blue Nun.

'How have you managed, dear?'

'Managed?' Joanie said, puzzled. 'I've

managed fine. How do you mean?'

They were both at the sink, Mary washing up and Joanie drying the dishes. Mary, her arms plunged into the foamy depths of the sink, stopped and turned to look at her niece.

'I sensed there was something that had upset you at the wedding, more so than the wedding itself. You were very quiet when we came back from the reception and, knowing you, I could not help but feel you were bottling something up. Am I right?'

Joanie found she could not meet her aunt's gaze without feeling the tears beginning to well up. Mary swiftly took Joanie's dishcloth from her and, having wiped the foamy washing up liquid from her hands, took her beloved niece in her arms, in an embrace that encompassed love and comfort all in one go.

'Who's hurt you, darling?' she whispered. 'Tell me.' She didn't add 'I'll make it better,' which she used to say when Joanie was a child. Then it was easier to put things right — most things, that is — but what was happening now no-one could fix.

Joanie gently eased herself out of her aunt's embrace.

'I'm fine,' she said, weakly.

'You're obviously not, dear. I can tell. Is it something to do with Martin, or perhaps your mother getting married again has upset you more than you think? What is it, Joanie? I can help.'

Though she felt it, Joanie didn't want to say, 'No-one can help me.' It would be too melodramatic, even if it was close to the truth because, actually, the only one who could help her was herself.

She needed to be stronger, more assertive. By running her own business she thought that that showed confidence enough in herself but she was still, under the skin, a child whose mother had denied her the love, affection and security that she should have been entitled to, which even Auntie Mary's true affection for her could not completely replace.

'Really, I'm fine, Auntie. I'm just tired. It's been a bit hectic in the shop, and then to come home and have to cook my own dinner . . . ' She was trying desperately to lighten the mood, to divert her aunt's gaze and attention away from her.

'You need an early night, then. Go on, go up and get into bed. I'll bring you a mug of Ovaltine in a little while like I did when you were a little girl.'

Mary's heart was aching with love and sympathy for this person who she'd always thought of as 'my little girl' but could never say it, feeling it would be wrong to deny her sister, Celia, the chance to come and claim Joanie one day and give her that love which only a mother truly can.

The thing was, nobody was expecting or waiting for it any more, which made it all the more sad.

Up, Up and Away

Martin seemed never to be at home any more, other than to change, have a bath and occasionally collect any mail that might be waiting for him. As far as this was concerned there was never ever anything of interest in the post. In his imagination he'd hoped — without any right or reason to — that there would, one day, be a letter from Joanie in amongst all the detritus, a letter which would explain and put everything right.

Of course this, like the recurring dream he had been having where an actual letter did turn up, was something that could not possibly or reasonably happen. For one thing, why write when you're both on the phone, and, secondly, what would she have to say?

He still felt angry, both with Joanie but also with himself at the way he'd behaved at the wedding reception, over a month ago now. How time flies, even when you're not enjoying yourself.

Before that day, August the fourth, he was already picturing himself and Joanie spending the rest of their lives together. Now look at us, he thought, bitterly. The trouble was, he had no-one to tell his troubles to — not his father, not his mother, not his sister, not even Jackie the air stewardess who'd been showing an interest in him, having been working the same couple of flights that Martin had been piloting just recently.

She was good company, not unattractive, either, but ever since Joanie, Martin had found that he could not commit himself into a relationship. It would be like a betrayal, ridiculous as that must seem, given that he and Joanie had not spoken or even caught sight of one another in the time since that awful day.

But Jackie was a nice girl. Besides, in this summer of love everyone seemed to be having a good time, so why shouldn't he?

★ ★ ★

After the emotional episode at the kitchen sink the previous week Joanie suddenly made the decision to move out. It was partly prompted by her landlord offering, out of the blue, the unoccupied flat above her shop. He'd seen stories in the newspapers of squatters taking over empty premises, and the law unable to do anything to prevent it or remove them.

Finding herself in a strong bargaining position regarding the terms and conditions, due to his fears for the vacant flat, Joanie got herself a good deal. The only problem was Aunt Mary.

'Are you sure, dear? It seems such a big step to take.'

'It's not really, Auntie. I virtually live there as it is. It's no big deal. And I'll still come and see you, of course I will.'

'I hope so, Joanie.'

It was as if Joanie was building a ring of steel around herself, so that no-one could either hurt her or expose her vulnerability. Her independence had suddenly become important to her, as a means of putting her destiny and her future solely in her own hands.

Actually living there, however, was a different story. Joanie had only ever known this part of London by day, when it was a busy, bustling, noisy area.

Sitting in her living-room, once her evening meal was done — thank goodness once again for Vesta — she found the quietness a bit unreal and a bit unnerving. It made her feel like a castaway.

Somewhere else — not here — life was carrying on, people were meeting, socialising, falling in love. The reality of what she had committed herself to was slowly sinking in. She felt, by signing a six-month lease, she'd burnt her bridges and had sentenced herself to 26 weeks of solitary confinement. Too much time on her hands, too much time to think, to recall, to remember things you'd much rather forget.

With sudden determination she stood up and went over to the small table that housed the phone. She picked up the directory and went through it looking for one person in particular.

She lifted the handset and began to dial.

Let the Good Times Roll

'I must say you took me by surprise, ringing me up out of the blue. But I'm glad you did. This is fun.'

Sue Parsons did seem genuinely pleased — now — that Joanie had telephoned her to ask her out for a drink. Surprised, as she said, but pleased.

'I felt I was a bit rude last time we met,' Joanie said, by way of explanation, 'and wanted to put things right.'

They were seated at a table in a themed bar of a Berni Inn; the theme, judging by the prints all around the walls, having some vague connection with music halls and Dame Nelly Melba. The restaurant was ideal as a halfway meet between the two young women, who seemed, so far, to be getting on well together.

'I didn't think you were rude, Jean. Sorry, I'm going to have trouble calling you Joanie. You've always been Jean to me, but I quite understand why you felt the need to change your name.'

She didn't, actually, because Joanie had only given the reason — partly true — that her present name fitted better with the whole concept of what she did for a living. That was enough for the time being.

Joanie still wasn't sure whether or not this had been a good idea. She could hardly remember Sue from school. It was just that she seemed to be on Joanie's side in a way that she had only experienced from a relative, her aunt. Martin no longer fitted into this equation, although he had made it painfully obvious that he was very clearly — and instantly — on opposing sides to her now.

'So what do you do for a living, then?' Joanie asked.

Sue grinned.

'Well, as I was one of those girls who always sat at the front in class I became, as you can imagine, a chartered accountant, eventually. Not exactly the image for a young girl in the Swinging Sixties.'

'We all need accountants, Sue.'

'I suppose that's true,' Sue said,

encouraged. Then she swiftly changed the subject. 'What did you see that time in the Wimpy bar that so upset you?'

'Oh, it was nothing, really. I thought I saw someone I knew.'

Sue frowned.

'How would that upset you? Was it an old boyfriend? I mean, I couldn't tell what it was — you were just staring out at what appeared to me to be just a crowd of people in Oxford Street.'

'It's complicated. Let's just say the person I saw wasn't who I thought he was. Let's leave it at that, shall we?'

There was an awkward silence that followed. Then, once again, Joanie's conscience pricked her.

'Sorry, Sue, I didn't mean to be short with you. It's just . . . '

'That's all right,' Sue said, with a genuine warmth in her voice which almost had Joanie crying.

What is wrong with me? You ask someone out you vaguely knew from school and then start behaving like an adolescent. Grow up!

'Anyway,' Joanie said, recovering her composure. 'What do you plan to do with the rest of your life?'

It almost sounded patronising, which it wasn't meant to, but Sue didn't seem to notice, taking the question on face value.

'Well, obviously I'd like to get married one day, have a family, you know. But, hey, who knows. As the song goes, 'Que Sera Sera', whatever will be will be.'

A sad expression seemed to spread across Sue's face and it looked like it was her turn to fight back the tears.

Joanie wondered if it was connected to that 'someone' she'd mentioned on their previous meeting, who had died.

'My sister,' she now said, 'was in her first year at university a year or so back. My parents were very proud of her. She was the first in our family to get into uni. Things seemed to be going well until she came home one weekend and told me she was pregnant.

'Since I saw you last she's had the baby, a beautiful little boy she called

John, after my boyfriend who'd died in a motorbike accident.'

She paused, appearing to collate all the facts and events surrounding this monumental event before clearing her throat a little and continuing.

'My parents were pretty horrified by it all and Sheila — that's my sister's name — went into what they call an unmarried mothers' home to have the baby.'

'So, what happened, after the baby was born?'

'He was put up for adoption. Sheila came home, and no-one ever mentioned John or anything surrounding him again. A month or so afterwards Sheila was allowed back at university, so everything is back to normal; except of course it isn't.' She shifted her position on the upholstered chair.

'The reason I'm saying all this is because I've had to stand back and watch those I had loved or would have loved, given the chance, taken away, and all the while the world just keeps on going as if nothing has happened.' She leant across and, like Auntie Mary sometimes did, put her hand on Joanie's arm.

'I don't know what it is that's hurting you, Joanie, but I can tell that someone or something has made you sad when you should be happy.' She looked at her watch, and then stood up.

'I've got to go, I'm afraid. I hope we meet again. Like I said, you always were someone special in my estimation and I'd like to think we could remain friends.'

Joanie stood up, too.

'I'd like that very much, too,' and she gave Sue a big hug before they went their separate ways.

Even the Bad Times are Good

September came, with just a hint of cooler days and longer nights. Joanie was getting well established in her new home. She'd also bought herself a second-hand car.

The telephone was a great comfort. She and her aunt would talk every evening on it, making their separation from one another less evident.

She would even talk to Sue at times. Ever since they'd last met, Joanie had felt a sort of bond develop between them. Sue said little but understood a lot. They were growing together like sisters, an experience Joanie had not known was possible till now.

The days were keeping her busy again. Now that the schools were back and the summer holidays were at an end she noticed a steady and increasing stream of potential purchasers.

All would have been good — perfect, even — if it were not for that continuing, dull ache in her heart.

Time is a great healer, they say, but too often in the evenings, time hung heavy, reminding her of what might have been and what could never be.

Sometimes she wondered what Martin was doing at those moments but, of course, it brought her no comfort. He, being the jet setting airline pilot, would have no problem finding someone to replace Joanie in his affections. But she tried to remain positive, even when on one particular Saturday afternoon she received a telephone call from Anthony at Passion For Fashion.

'Hi, Joanie, sorry I haven't been in touch. How are you? I'm pretty good, you know, busy and all that. Just wondered whether you fancied coming out tonight. A mate of mine is throwing a housewarming party. He's got this really cool apartment by the river. What d'you reckon? You up for it?'

Despite her misgivings about Anthony

and his somewhat dubious business practices, Joanie thought it would do her good to get out, meet some new people and, hopefully, just enjoy herself. She just had one question.

'Can I bring a friend?'

'Depends,' Anthony said, on his guard. 'Chick or guy?'

Joanie was momentarily confused. Chick? The person she had in mind didn't exactly come under the definition of chick, but she recovered — and remembered — quickly enough to give her answer.

Martin wasn't exactly enjoying himself in the cocktail bar that Jackie had persuaded him to take her to. Try as he might — and Jackie didn't think much of his efforts, so far — to please, his heart wasn't in it.

He had hoped that, by dating someone else, he would be able to release himself from the continuing feelings he still held for Joanie. Why won't she leave me alone, he thought, not accepting that, actually, it was down to him to move on and put her out of his mind.

Simple enough, but for the fact that she still held his heart hostage which, despite the way he had spoken to her at his father's wedding reception, he was unable to be free himself from those feelings of both love and loss.

'Get me another one, will you, darling.' Jackie tried to look coquettish as she pushed her empty glass towards Martin. He didn't much care for that, nor the over-familiarity of her terms of endearment. He wasn't anyone's darling, yet how could he stop her without seeming unkind or hurtful.

It wasn't Jackie's fault he wasn't in love with her. How could he be, and how could she know? How could he ever explain to anyone what was going on in his head when he could hardly make sense of it himself.

'Why don't we go back to my place instead?' he suddenly suggested. Not the best idea but, at the moment, it seemed a better option than staying in this place.

Jackie's eyes lit up. She didn't need

121

asking twice.

'Sounds good to me,' she said, grabbing her bag and, quickly locking her arm through his, guided him out of the bar before he might have a chance to change his mind.

They drove back through the quiet streets with the hood down, Jackie's long brown hair flowing freely behind her as they sped along.

Martin glanced across at her. There was no doubt she was attractive and . . . who knows, maybe things would work out OK for them both, one day.

★　★　★

'I hope you girls are enjoying yourselves. Can I get you another drink?' Anthony offered.

Both Joanie and Sue put their hands over their glasses.

'No, thanks.' Joanie smiled.

'But we are having a good time, yes,' Sue added, apparently out of politeness rather than conviction.

'Well, how's about we have a little dance, Joanie?'

'Sure, later. I'm just enjoying being here. This place is fabulous.'

It was true. Joanie had been briefly introduced to Anthony's friend, Paul, who owned the apartment and whose party it was, and she was amazed at its position and its décor and furniture.

It seemed to contain everything that both Habitat and Liberty had to offer with one or two bespoke additions, like, for example, an Eero Aarnio white fibreglass swivel ball chair and a glass-topped coffee table supported by two Rolls Royce grills, apparently designed by Ringo Starr.

Sue was even more astonished by all these opulent trappings.

'Who is the feller who owns all this?' she asked Joanie, hoping for some clarification.

'I think he owns all those Beyond The Pale stores; I believe there's one in Knightsbridge as well as Oxford Street and Carnaby Street, plus he's got a concession inside Selfridges.'

'Wow, he must be worth a fortune.'

They walked from room to room, between the other party guests, taking it all in. Whether Sue was thinking the same as Joanie was not clear, but Joanie herself found she was subconsciously making comparisons to her own little flat, and they were not favourable.

Anthony reappeared in front of them.

'What about that dance, then?' he said, looking directly at Joanie.

'I'm sorry, Anthony, it's just I've been on my feet all day and I'd prefer to sit down in one of those lovely armchairs. But I'm sure Sue would like to dance with you.'

There was a moment's hesitation from Anthony as his eyes switched from the naturally beautiful Joanie to the not so obviously attractive Sue who now began messing around with her hair under Anthony's scrutiny.

'Yeah, right,' he said. 'Come on then, Sal . . . '

'It's Sue, actually,' she said, as he

pulled her into the centre of the sitting-room where the dancing was taking place. Whatever else she might have been saying was lost in that vortex of moving people to the opening bars of 'Soul Man' by Sam and Dave.

Joanie would have loved to have danced but just not with Anthony. She would also loved to have sat in the ball chair but lacked the nerve to do so. So, instead, she sat down in one of the sumptuous leather recliners, closed her eyes and wished herself away.

★ ★ ★

'Would you like a coffee?' Martin asked, as Jackie prowled around his small flat, like a cat.

'Depends what you've got to go in it.' She had finally come to rest in his bedroom. Something, on his bedside table, caught her eye. 'Is this for me?' she called out, after a while.

'Is what for you?' Martin called back, sorting out the coffees.

'This.' She had silently tip-toed into the kitchen. Martin turned round. Jackie was right up close to him — too close — and in her hand she was holding a small hinged box.

A Whiter Shade of Pale

Although Joanie's mother had been back from her honeymoon for nearly a month now, the only contact she had made was to her sister, Mary. She'd telephoned briefly to ask, 'Who was that man who was at our wedding? I'd never seen him before and neither had Henry. When I sent the invitation out to Jean it was assumed that you would be the one accompanying her.'

'He was a friend — an old friend from my youth. I didn't think you would mind.'

'I didn't say I minded,' Celia replied testily. 'I just had no idea you would be bringing someone I didn't know.'

Mary took a deep breath, apprehensive at what she was about to say.

'Well, Celia, you do know him, actually.'

'I think you must be mistaken, Mary. I've never seen him before in my life. What's his name?'

'Ray, Ray Compton. Now do you

remember?'

There was a perceptible silence on the other end of the line, as Mary's words slowly began to sink in.

'Wasn't he that man you were engaged to?' Celia eventually said. 'I thought he was killed, somewhere over France, wasn't it?'

'We were never engaged and, yes, we all assumed he'd been killed, but he wasn't.'

'Well then, why didn't he come back and find you? I don't understand.'

In some ways neither did Mary. Celia's probing, awkward questions had sown similar doubts and questions in her own mind. But she was determined not to let it cloud her judgement now.

As she'd told herself a hundred times, the past is past, there is nothing we can do to change it, only try to make the most of what we have now. But it would be very difficult to persuade her sister to share that philosophy.

'It's too complicated to explain. I'm just happy that we are back in touch again. It was really nice to see him after all this time.'

'If you say so.' Celia was unconvinced, but she had other things on her mind. 'I have some news. Henry's son has become engaged. Henry's really pleased and the lady in question, Jackie, seems very pleasant. It seems my marrying Henry has inspired his son to also decide to settle down.'

Mary didn't know what to say, other than the usual congratulations. It was hardly of any interest to her; she wasn't even aware that Henry had a son. No-one had mentioned him before.

'Anyway, I thought you'd be interested to know, Mary.'

'Yes, Celia, that's very good news. Congratulations,' she said again.

There was silence on the line.

'Mary? Are you still there? It's gone very quiet. Mary?'

'Yes, I'm still here. By the way,' she added, trying to interest Celia in her own daughter, 'I thought Jean looked very pretty. She designed and made that trouser suit herself, you know.'

'Did she?' Celia replied. 'I don't know why girls these days want to cover their legs in trousers, especially for such an occasion.'

'That's the fashion, Celia. And being a fashion designer it's only right she should be wearing the latest trends, don't you agree?'

'I'm sure I don't know. Anyway, I've told you what I had to say. Goodbye.'

And before Mary had time to respond the line had gone dead. She remained where she was, sitting down, the receiver cradled in her lap, trying, yet again, to come to terms with her sister's cold indifference towards her daughter.

As much as I love Joanie, I know it should be Celia feeling the love and compassion for her before me. She sighed. Some things in this life seemed very cruel. What could be so difficult in loving a girl who had nothing but love to give back?

It was a mystery to Mary, and one, which at times like this, she didn't think was ever going to be solved.

She put the handset back, but remained seated by the table. She felt a sort of spiritual despair at not being able to do anything that might change matters.

* * *

Henry Smythe had arranged to meet his son, Martin, at his club in Mayfair. He was feeling somewhat nervous at the prospect which, he acknowledged to himself, was a pretty poor state of affairs, but given the current circumstances, he felt he needed to clear the air between father and son, and the only way to do it with any hope of a happy outcome was to meet away from home.

As usual, he arrived way too early. He was a stickler for punctuality, but today he would rather not have had any more time on his hands. He wanted to get down to it, get it sorted, but the longer he was having to wait the less assured he became of his own ability to say what needed to be said.

Uncharacteristically, at this time of the morning, he ordered for himself a brandy, something that didn't pass unnoticed by the long-serving waiter who took his order.

'There you are, sir,' the waiter said, proffering the drink on a small silver salver. 'I trust all is well, Mr Smythe.'

'Fine, thank you, Timothy. Purely medicinal, purely medicinal.' In a sense it was true. Henry felt he needed something to calm the butterflies in his stomach. He was worrying as to how Martin was going to react to what he had to say. Had to say? Why should I — of all people — think that I can give advice on the matter?

A few minutes later, Martin arrived. He looked tired and preoccupied, and refused the offer of a drink, even coffee.

'What's this about, Dad?' he wanted to know, sitting only on the edge of the seat opposite his father, rather as if he were ready to take off at any moment.

'Thanks for coming, Martin. How's

things?'

'Fine, fine,' Martin replied with a touch of impatience. 'You said you wanted to see me.'

'Yes.' He paused for so long that Martin had to press for an answer. 'Yes, I'm sorry, son, I just don't know how to put this. Your news, about your getting engaged, came as a bit of a . . . surprise to us . . .'

'Us? You haven't spoken to Mother, have you?'

'Good heavens, no, although I imagine she's delighted for you — for you both.'

'Not in the least,' Martin said. 'She's tried everything in her power to put me off the idea of marriage. And I can see why she would.'

Henry looked genuinely puzzled.

'Can you? Why?'

'Well, it's obvious, isn't it? After you were unfaithful to her she's hardly going to see marriage as something to aspire to. She's never got over it, you know.'

Henry sighed and looked down into his empty glass. Something seemed to be troubling his conscience. To tell or not to tell . . . Finally, he looked up again.

'It really wasn't as straightforward as that,' he began.

★ ★ ★

'Where have you been?' Celia demanded of her husband, when he returned home shortly before lunch.

You, too, he thought, seeing the expression of suspicion on her face.

'I did say, dear, that I was going up to town to see Martin.'

Celia's face cleared. When she wasn't looking disapproving or suspicious she was actually very pretty. Even now, it was plain to Henry what her first husband must have seen in her, and when he and Celia had met at the book fair in town over a year ago, her charm and elegant demeanour had completely besotted him.

It was just that, since their marriage, she seemed . . . what was the word . . . neurotic? Yes, that was it, neurotic.

And being like that wasn't doing her any favours. It didn't help him that they continued to live in Celia's house where the ghost of her dead husband often seemed to be an invisible factor in their relationship.

What we need is our own place where we can begin making our own memories without someone else's presence coming between us.

'I'm just going into the study, dear,' he said.

Celia glanced at her watch.

'Don't be long. Lunch will be at one o'clock sharp.'

'I won't be.' He headed for the quiet sanctuary of the one room in the house he had laid claim to.

He closed the door quietly, then walked over to his desk, seating himself behind it in the wood and leather swivel chair. These two items of furniture he'd owned for almost all his adult life.

After his wartime service as a commissioned officer in the Royal Navy he went to work as a journalist and author for Jane's Fighting Ships, first at their offices and then, once his reputation had been established, from home.

It was all, he realised now, that he had as a material possession that connected him to his past life and family. Not much to show for those years. Less, in fact, than some even knew.

As he sat in the chair, rocking slowly to and fro, feeling a bit like a pendulum passing away time that could never come back or be made good, he considered whether he'd done the right thing telling Martin the truth; the truth about the cause and circumstance in the break-up of Henry's marriage, and the even harsher truth concerning Martin himself.

At first Martin refused to believe either version of events that Henry had — very reluctantly — told him.

'You expect me to believe that? Mother has always blamed you. You were the one who had the affair — you were the one who left her in the lurch.'

'I know it looks that way,' Henry had

said, 'but that's not how it was.'

'What do you mean?'

'It was your mother who had the affair, Martin, not me.'

Martin was becoming visibly distressed by Henry's claim and went to stand up as if he were going to leave. Henry reached across to try and prevent him but was shaken off. However, Martin did not go. He remained to hear the whole shocking, distressing, true story.

'I loved your mother, Martin, but she didn't, I discovered, actually love me. The war, you know, blurred things, made you make decisions you might not, in more settled, peaceful times, have made.

'I had been courting her for a couple of years and everyone was expecting that we would, eventually, get married. I thought we might wait till the war was over but your mother seemed quite insistent which I didn't — stupidly — understand at the time.

'Then it all made sense. Seven months after we were wed you were born. I knew then why the urgency, why the need for a wedding ring.'

'What are you saying?'

'I'm saying, Martin, that I have always loved you as if you were my own flesh and blood, no more or less than Paula. But, of course, the sad fact is you're not technically my son.'

'Why are you telling me all this? And why should I believe you?'

'Because it's the truth. And I have nothing to gain by lying. Besides, I don't want to see you getting married to someone you don't love and who doesn't love you.'

Martin had no answer to that. He wasn't even sure how he'd got himself into that situation. It seemed that Jackie, once she'd discovered the engagement ring on Martin's bedside table, engineered the next moves.

And for some reason due to, maybe, the sad loneliness he was feeling as a result of not being with Joanie any more, he'd allowed himself to be persuaded into agreeing to the engagement.

It had given him, if only briefly, a feeling

of self-worth. It was comforting — like a warm, glowing fire in winter — to feel loved, that someone should want him, exclusively, absolutely.

The trouble with a fire, though, is if you don't keep adding to the flames it will go out, and then everywhere becomes cold again, which is how Martin felt now despite his best efforts to deny it.

Henry, remembering the morning's conversation, was overcome with a fear that, by confiding in his son, he had lost his trust and affection for ever.

'But you were the one cited in the divorce,' Martin had said, trying to restore the fault and blame back on to this man he had always thought was his father.

'I know, Martin. I agreed to it because your mother had — has — some significant standing in the community, and people tend to judge women far more harshly than they do men. And it was easy enough to arrange.'

'But why divorce at all? You must have been reasonably happy, or is Paula not yours, either?'

'Of course she is. No, Martin, I tried my best but I'm afraid your mother never really loved me. I think her heart belonged to whoever it was who was your actual father.

'I am truly sorry that I have to tell you this but it's because I dread the thought of you marrying someone you're not in love with.'

'And are you in love now, with Celia?'

'I am, yes. Oh, I know she comes across as a bit standoffish at times but she has always shown me a depth of fondness that I'd never known with your mother.' Henry, feeling desperately sorry for having upset Martin, leaned across and patted his arm. This time Martin did not draw away. He just remained seated, silent, and bewildered by all that he had been told.

I Never Loved a Man (The Way I Love You)

Joanie was pleased and yet at the same time secretly jealous. Her new friend Sue had surprised her by actually getting together with Anthony at the party they'd all recently attended. Now they were a couple.

'I've not felt like this for a long time, Joanie. I never thought it could happen again.'

They were having one of their regular telephone conversations — although, just lately, they were anything but regular, as Joanie struggled to find Sue in these days, which, unwittingly, added to her own feelings of discontent and loneliness — not that she'd ever let on to Sue that that was how she was feeling.

'I know he's not perfect,' Sue went on, in an enthusiastic way which suggested he actually was perfect, 'but he makes me happy, Joanie — he makes me laugh.

I'm so pleased you and I met up, otherwise I'd never have met Anthony.'

'I'm really pleased for you,' Joanie said, trying to match her friend's enthusiasm, but it was an uphill struggle. 'I'd best go, otherwise my dinner will be ruined.'

'What you having?'

Joanie wasn't expecting this and so had to think fast.

'I'm making a paella,' she explained, which was true in the fact that it was a paella, just not one she was having to make unless you call emptying a packet into a saucepan of hot water and stirring occasionally, as 'making'.

'We will meet up soon, Joanie, I promise. Bye for now.'

'Bye.'

The aroma of the paella filled the room, its smell suggesting something so much more exotic than a meal for one in an upstairs bedsit.

Joanie sighed. She seemed to do a lot of sighing these days, something which only she ever heard. Sometimes she wondered if she'd been a bit too hasty in moving out from her aunt's comfort-able — comforting — house. Or would she feel lonely wherever she was? Only in her shop — as long as it was busy — did her mind free itself from what her heart was feeling, but Sundays and Mondays accentuated her isolation. I must snap out of this, she told herself on numerous occasions but, even as she tried to, a song would come on Radio Caroline to remind her of what she had lost.

The summer of love had become the autumn of discontent, and she didn't know how to change it.

★ ★ ★

Martin was in a daze. He could not believe what his father had told him, yet he had no reason to doubt him. Henry, whom he'd loved and respected until his mother had divorced him, was not to blame, did not deserve the hidden resentment that both he and his sister, Paula, had nurtured.

But it was all too unbelievable! And

none of this would have come to light if he — Martin — had not got himself engaged to the manipulative Jackie.

He wondered how he could face her, wondered if she would be able to see, in his manner, his actions, that it was not love that he felt for her, just the transient feelings of desire. Henry had seen through the façade, so why not her?

And then there was his mother! How could he look her in the eye again without betraying what he now knew to be true.

Things will never be the same again, he thought. And this was even more true than all the rest of it put together.

If only he'd known this before — before it all went wrong at Joanie's mother's wedding reception. How arrogant and bigoted he must have seemed, and how cuttingly cruel he was to have said those things. There's nothing I can do about it now. I expect she's found someone else, like I have, apparently.

★ ★ ★

It seemed that Joanie was the only one who hadn't found someone else. Even her friend, Sue, was moving further ahead, and therefore further away from her.

'He wants me to go and live with him, Joanie,' she said excitedly one evening on the telephone.

'And how do you feel about that?' Joanie had sensed a tone of anxiousness, despite the excitement in her friend's voice.

'I'm not sure. I don't think my parents would be too pleased. But . . . '

'But what?'

'I do believe I love him, Joanie, and I do so much want to be with him, all the time. And I mean all the time.'

'Does he love you?'

There was a significant pause.

'I think so,' Sue said, with uncertainty.

Joanie felt she should not interfere.

'Just see how it goes,' was all she could offer. After all, who was she to hand out advice? She wasn't even able to give herself advice concerning matters of the heart.

As September neared its end, Joanie found herself busy enough with her shop not to have to think about love — and, in particular Martin — for, if not days, then hours at a time. His words, when she recalled them, still stung, but she tried her best to remain positive.

What she would have thought had she known that Martin was engaged is difficult to know. Pleased? Disappointed? Angry?

Fortunately for her it was of no interest to her mother, Celia, so there was little likelihood of her mentioning it to Joanie. And then Auntie Mary, having found the news of little interest, too, and not knowing the significant connection, had not bothered to pass it on. So Joanie carried on with her life, totally unaware.

As October began there was a change in the weather; a definite chill first and last thing. The early days were sunny enough, and reasonably warm, throwing everyone — not just Joanie — into

146

confusion as to what they should be wearing. Actually, Joanie knew what they ought to be dressed in at this time but sales were slack due to this unseasonably clement weather. Some days she had as few as half a dozen customers which made her begin to question her decision to go it alone in the highly fickle fashion industry.

'Things will pick up, you'll see,' Mary said, trying to be encouraging. It was Sunday and Joanie had invited herself round for lunch, much to her aunt's delight.

'I wish I shared your confidence, Auntie,' Joanie replied. 'I sometimes think it would be easier to give it all up and go and work for someone else, let them worry about sales and such.'

'I'm sure you're not serious, dear. A week or so from now you'll be so busy you'll wonder why you ever considered the idea.'

'I hope you're right.'

You Keep Me Hanging On

After Joanie had left, Mary sat down at the kitchen table, pondering her dilemma. She had been intending to tell her niece what Ray had suggested but somehow the right moment never seemed to arise.

His letter had come a few days previously containing the offer. Part of her wanted to accept but, equally, she could see that it would cause difficulties.

The situation was unique, unprecedented. She and Joanie had always spent Christmas together. It would be hard to imagine it any other way. But, of course, nothing stays the same. Things happen, and it would have been nice to visit Ray in France, to meet his daughter and son, and to experience, for a while, what life might have been like for herself.

I wish I knew what was right, she thought.

★ ★ ★

'I think we ought to get married in a church, darling. What do you say?'

Jackie was seated on the end of Martin's bed, idly flicking through the pages of 'Brides' magazine.

Ever since Martin had found himself agreeing to marrying Jackie she seemed to have nothing else to talk about and he was rapidly tiring of it. He also found that several of her idiosyncrasies were beginning to irritate him.

Even now, as he glanced across at her from the open kitchen, the way she kept coiling her hair back over her ear as she looked down at the photos, jarred with him.

Perhaps I'm looking for things to find fault with her, he thought. It was his own fault if he did, he had to acknowledge. He could have said no when she confronted him with the engagement ring — the engagement ring which he'd bought for Joanie.

Even thinking her name made him sigh inwardly. How could things have gone from that to this in such a short

149

time? Why was he so weak?

She seemed to have no other aspiration these days than to be a bride. She'd probably not given a thought to anything else other than the venue, the honeymoon and the outfits she would require.

Female emancipation had gone right over her head.

Of course, her family had some influence in this respect. Her father was a leading barrister whose wife did not go to work.

Instead she involved herself in the running of their household and of serving on a variety of local organisations, such as the WI and the League Of Friends. Martin was not critical of them but he could see that it gave Jackie an over-inflated sense of her own importance as well as a narrow-minded point of view of life in the second half of the 20th century.

'And the honeymoon, Martin. Any ideas?'

'We should probably stay somewhere in England, don't you think? We've been just about everywhere in the world but I don't think I've ever had any sort of holiday in the UK.'

Jackie gave him a withering look.

'If you think I'm going to go to all that trouble,' she said, holding up the 'Brides' magazine, 'just to spend my honeymoon in West Wittering, well then, all I can say is, think again.'

'I certainly will,' Martin said, looking at Jackie as she turned back to the pages of her magazine. 'I certainly will.'

Daydream Believer

Joanie was getting the shop ready for Christmas. She loved the build up to it, despite the fact that her childhood lacked the parents and any siblings to make it memorable.

Auntie Mary had always done her best. The food was delicious and, where she would have been so busy in the shop, it was always nice for Joanie to be able to put her feet up and relax before the January sales began.

Also, around this time, she wished she'd taken on an extra pair of hands to help her, but she could never, somehow, allow herself to let go of the reins at all. The shop was her baby and a lot of the clothes being sold had her work and name imprinted on it.

She wanted to be there when a purchase was made, to see the look on the customer's face, to hear what they might have to say about what they'd just bought. It was as if she was handing over part of herself — not quite the same as handing over a baby, but there was that connection for Joanie, making it all the more incomprehensible to her how her mother could so easily have handed her over, even into the safe and loving arms of her aunt.

But she wouldn't dwell on these negative thoughts. She wanted Christmas to be a happy time.

She'd even — almost — managed to put Martin out of her mind, sometimes for days at a time. She still liked to imagine that it had all been a bad dream and that, soon, he would come walking through that door again, all smiles and affection, to take her in his arms and tell her again what he'd once told her — that he loved her, loved her as much as she'd loved him.

But it was all past tense now and as such it needed to stay there. In just over a month it would be a new year, and then she could set her eyes firmly on the future — a clean slate.

Martin was attending yet another tedious drinks party. He could hardly believe how many 'friends' Jackie had. This one, however, was a little bit different from the rest as it happened to be Martin's boss who was hosting it. Simon Reeds loved to show off his luxury apartment in a better part of London, with its view of the flowing Thames and St Paul's Cathedral.

'That's my parish church,' he would tell everyone whenever they were summoned for drinks. There was seldom a danger of his repeating himself, owing to the fact that most people usually didn't come again.

And, of course, it was always 'just drinks' at his place. He had no regular partner so was not in any way domesticated enough to offer anything more than peanuts or crisps to go along with the liquid refreshment.

Still, Jackie seemed to be enjoying herself. She relished the luxuriousness of it all, and Simon was happy enough to mention all the right names when describing a piece of furniture or artefact around the place.

'Yes, that's one of Conran's better pieces,' he casually remarked, pointing to one of the settees.

'It's gorgeous,' Jackie rightfully responded.

'Yes, and so is the bedroom suite.' He was openly smirking as he said this. 'Maybe you'd like to see for yourself.'

'I'd love to.' Jackie smiled sweetly back, reminding Martin, who had all the time been watching, of Fenella Fielding. Jackie caught his eye and immediately adopted a more demure pose. 'Maybe later,' she whispered, as she walked back to her fiancé.

'You seem to be enjoying yourself,' Martin said. He should, he supposed, have felt jealous, seeing the two of them together openly flirting. But he felt nothing. He couldn't have cared less, which was wrong, he knew.

'No thanks to you.' She pouted. 'Get

me a drink, will you?'

'Glad to.' He went off to do so but it took a while to be served at the make-shift bar. When he returned, Jackie was nowhere to be found. And, significantly, neither was Simon.

* * *

Mary felt she had made a decision which would accommodate everyone. She hadn't as yet discussed it with Joanie but she was quite hopeful it wouldn't upset her. As long as they could all spend Christmas together then she felt she would be justified in going over to France for New Year.

She just hoped that Ray's son and daughter would agree to come. Fortunately, the farm they all worked on was arable so there wasn't the need for some-one to be in attendance all day every day at this time of year.

Mary couldn't explain to herself why she thought it was so important that Ray should bring his children with them, she just knew, somehow, that it mattered.

Not that they were children any more. The daughter was nineteen or so and the son was coming up for seventeen. Obviously it must have been devastating for them both — at any age — to have lost their mother, and Mary had no intention of trying to act as a surrogate to them. It was just that she thought that if she could overcome her own feelings of loss, then she might be able to share the compassion that Ray's children probably still needed.

If only she could be certain how everyone would be in the circumstances. In her imagination it was going to be a Christmas to remember — for all the right reasons. It was just a shame that Celia wasn't willing — or able — to share in it, too.

Night of Fear

'You should go, Auntie, you'll enjoy it.'

'I haven't been asked yet, Joanie.'

It was Sunday. The two women were in their usual chairs, either side of the fireplace. A log fire was burning fiercely in the grate, the weather having turned bitterly cold in the last few days.

'But they're coming here for Christmas, aren't they?'

'Yes. I was pleased to hear they'd agreed to that.'

'Why wouldn't they? You always do an amazing Christmas dinner and this house is spacious enough for everyone not to get in each other's way. It will be brilliant.'

Mary was pleased, but at the same time puzzled by Joanie's apparent endorsement of her plans for Christmas and New Year.

'Won't you be a bit lonely?' she asked, concerned and not fooled by her niece's upbeat manner.

'I'll be fine, Auntie. I've got my sale starting on the second, and it will keep me busy getting everything ready for it. You really mustn't worry about me, I'm telling you, I'll be fine.'

Keep me busy.

Both aunt and niece had picked up on this phrase which Joanie had used, and it only helped to make Mary even more concerned at the prospect of going to France to see the new year in.

Joanie, too, was aware of what she'd said. It seemed the only way to try to put Martin out of her mind was to 'keep busy.'

Had she been aware of his present circumstances her heart and mind might have taken on a different — and less sorrowful — attitude.

* * *

The phone call came shortly before midnight. Joanie had long gone home and Mary was in bed — though not asleep — when it rang, causing alarm bells of her own to ring at its sound so late at night.

'Is that Miss Mary Saunders?' an unknown female voice asked when Mary picked up the receiver, having hurried downstairs to do so.

'Yes. Who is this?'

'My name is Sister Lloyd. I'm at the west end central hospital. Are you the sister of Mrs Celia Smythe?'

Panic was taking over. Mary's heart was pounding.

'I am. What's happened to her?'

'I can't say much over the telephone, except that she and her husband were involved in a road traffic accident earlier this evening. Are you able to get here?'

'How bad is it?'

'Your sister is in a critical condition. I can't tell you any more than that. The doctor in charge will explain in more detail when you get here.'

Mary felt numb. Quickly she got dressed, all the while wondering should she tell Joanie? But why shouldn't she know? She was her mother after all, despite everything. Yet she hesitated. There was still that almost instinctive need to protect Joanie, particularly where it concerned her mother.

Perhaps I'll wait till I get to the hospital, and find out just how serious it is, she thought, and then immediately doubted the notion.

★　★　★

Joanie was dreaming. In her dream she was walking through her shop which seemed to go on and on until someone came forward from behind a rail of jackets, holding a telephone in her hands.

There was something vaguely familiar about the person, a girl of similar age to herself but dressed in a nightgown similar to those worn in hospitals. Joanie began to remember who it was she reminded her of, that girl who came peering into her shop back in the spring.

'You have a message,' the spectre said, holding the phone out to her, at which point Joanie woke up, roused by her actual telephone in the kitchen/diner. She looked at the clock on her bedside table. Twenty-past twelve. Who on earth could be ringing at this time of night?

As soon as she'd heard her aunt's voice she rapidly got dressed and rushed downstairs, through the shop and out into her car.

★ ★ ★

Martin had not gone to bed when the call came through to him. It was not the hospital calling, however, but his sister.

'Martin, Father's had an accident, he's in hospital.'

'How badly hurt is he?'

'He's broken his leg and fractured his ribs.'

'How did it happen?'

'A car crash. I'm going over there in a while. Are you?'

'I will, yes. Was Celia with him?'

'Oh, yes. But they wouldn't tell me how she was.'

'I'm going now. Which hospital are

162

they in?'

As he drove through the deserted London streets he wondered whether Joanie would be there. She surely would, which could be awkward for them both. He sort of hoped that his father would already be in a men's ward so that there would be no possibility of their encountering one another.

The reception area of the hospital was deserted, and it took him a while to find anyone who could tell him where his father was. He had been admitted but wasn't in a ward.

'I believe he's with his wife in the intensive care unit.' The nurse pointed him in the direction of the unit before hurrying off to deal with another incoming casualty.

The corridors seemed endless in this place. Martin hurried through them, a heightened sense of inward panic propelling him.

Finally he reached the double doors that led into the intensive care unit and saw his father, seated in a wheelchair, one leg cast in plaster, alongside a bed in which the almost unrecognisable figure of his wife, Celia, lay, unconscious and with a network of tubes and machines attached to her still body.

The only sign that suggested she was still alive was the shallow, barely perceptible movements of her chest.

Martin stepped quietly across to stand next to his father whose face, peppered with small cuts and bruises, was ashen, his features etched with desperate anxiety and fear.

Martin, staring with silent horror at Celia, placed a hand gently on Henry's shoulder. His father never turned his head away from his wife but nodded an acknowledgement to his son.

'What are they saying?' Martin whispered.

Henry sighed.

'They can't say yet whether she will survive, or, if she does, whether there will be any permanent damage.'

Martin did not need to ask what the doctors meant by 'permanent damage'.

Just looking at Celia he found it hard to imagine that life was ever going to fully return to her. It was shocking, and heartbreaking for his father.

'What happened?'

Still without looking up, Henry answered his son's question.

'We were heading home when a car pulled out at speed from a side road. Celia took the most impact as it hit us on her side.' Tears welled up in his eyes. 'There was nothing I could do, Martin,' he added, shaking his head. 'It all happened so quickly.'

Martin squeezed his father's shoulder. But, continuing to look at Celia, he found that he did not have anything to say which could offer genuine comfort or hope.

* * *

Joanie, too, had been driving through the mainly deserted streets, going as fast as she dared towards the hospital. All sorts of terrifying thoughts were running

165

through her head and nothing was getting through which could offer anything positive to the appalling situation she was soon going to find herself in.

What if she dies, she kept thinking, not allowing her thoughts to go further than that. But it was there, at the back of her mind — a mother who had not loved her who might die without ever anything having changed.

And yet, here she was, in a near state of panic, driving somewhat recklessly towards the hospital, desperate for her to survive, desperate for another chance — for both of them — to be united in love as a mother and daughter truly should be.

Mary's taxi drew up outside the main entrance to the hospital only minutes before Joanie was about to arrive.

A kind nurse not only told her where to go but, seeing Mary's agitation, led her along the various corridors to the IC ward itself where they found Martin and Henry watching over the comatose figure of Celia.

Mary put her hand over her mouth to stifle any shocked outburst that might have been coming. Whilst Henry maintained his vigil, Martin turned and then walked across to where Mary stood, frozen, in the doorway.

He took her arm, steering her gently towards the bed.

'She's stable, they've said,' he told her, partly for Henry's benefit. Things were bad enough without Mary knowing the truth of the situation.

Mary, recovering, turned to Martin.

'Why are you here?'

'I'm Henry's son.'

A nurse, brisk, business-like, suddenly appeared.

'Doctor's coming to see her,' she said, nodding her head in the direction of the stricken patient. 'You'll all have to wait outside for the moment.'

She didn't wait to see them leave the room. She had every confidence in her manner and tone of voice, knowing that they, all three, would obey her instruction, which they duly did, Martin slowly

167

guiding his father's wheelchair out into the corridor. There were a few seats out here but no-one felt like sitting down.

After a few minutes a doctor, white coated and with a stethoscope hung round his neck, came out of a side door and began striding purposefully towards the anxious group.

Behind him followed the nurse who'd instructed the small party to exit the room. She seemed to be struggling to keep up with the middle-aged medic who now stopped briefly to acknowledge the presence of Celia's family.

'You can go back in when I've finished my examination,' he told them, not looking at anyone in particular.

It was as they were waiting for the doctor to carry out his examination that Joanie arrived. Her face was as white as the walls of the corridor she was walking down, which was partly due to the situation but also, now, because she'd just caught sight of Martin.

She felt as if her legs were going to give out on her and her heart started beating even faster. What would she say? What would he say? But would it matter anyway in these awful circumstances?

It was of no consequence as it happened. Before she even had a chance to ask how her mother was, the doctor reappeared in the corridor with the nurse in close attendance. He looked at each one of them with the same serious expression before speaking.

'There is no change,' he said, in very much a matter of fact tone. 'Her condition remains critical but stable. We shall keep monitoring her throughout the night. Any questions?'

Everyone had questions but they each of them knew that nobody — not even this doctor, with all his medical skills and knowledge — would be able to give them the answers they all craved . . . Will she get better?

Having waited politely for a moment or two, and receiving no response to his question, the doctor turned on his heel and marched off back down the corridor, the nurse, as before, struggling to keep up.

Martin was the first to move, taking hold of the handles of his father's wheelchair and then making a concentrated effort at steering it back through the doorway of the ward, never looking up or around him as he did so.

Funny Familiar Forgotten Feelings

They were taking it in turns to sit with Celia, alongside Henry, that is. He wouldn't leave her side even though he was obviously in pain himself. He disregarded all his own issues, focusing all his attention on his wife, willing her to regain consciousness.

That would be a start. Just to have her open her eyes, to see that those who love her are all here. It was the nearest he could bring himself to praying. He wanted to believe that faith could make miracles, but it was also clear enough that she required divine intervention to give her any chance of recovering.

Joanie and Martin may as well have been invisible to one another, although they were both perfectly aware of each other's existence. But it was difficult.

As the night ticked slowly on, and there were still no signs of any change in Celia, Joanie felt as if her head would explode. The anxiety of it all, the helplessness she felt at not being able to do anything herself to help her mother.

What surprised her — troubled her in some way — was how strong that invisible bond must be, if not between them, then from herself to her mother. She wanted so much to physically reach out and embrace her but the best she dared manage was to put her hand on hers, gently stroking it.

'You ought to get some rest, dear.' Mary had come over to the seated figure of her niece, putting a protective arm around the young woman's shoulder. She was still struggling to come to terms with the fact that Martin was Henry's son. And she'd never known! But surely there must be another son who was engaged to Jackie.

Joanie stared blankly up at her aunt.

'What if she never wakes up, Auntie?'

'We can't know, dear. And all the while she's got breath in her body we must keep hoping. Come with me, dear. Let's get a drink, at least.'

'What time is it?' Joanie asked as she slowly, reluctantly got to her feet.

Mary glanced at her watch.

'Five-fifty.'

Joanie left the room. As Mary followed she heard Henry speak to Martin.

'Do you think your fiancée should be told?'

Mary, her heart racing, didn't wait to hear Martin's response. Joanie was some way ahead, which she was grateful for, as she hoped it would give her time to regain her composure after what she'd just heard.

As Joanie walked along the corridor, a figure, at once familiar, yet unknown, came walking from the opposite direction. Passing each other, Joanie immediately realised it was the girl who'd come by her shop that day, therefore the girl walking along Oxford Street, possessively holding on to Martin's arm.

Joanie stopped, turned and watched the figure till she disappeared out of sight at the turn in the corridor.

Mary had by now caught up with her niece who continued to look back down the corridor where the girl had gone.

'Is something the matter, dear?'

'That girl, Auntie. She's the one I saw on Martin's arm in Oxford Street, I'm sure of it.'

'Jackie?' As soon as she'd said it, she wished she hadn't. A whole Pandora's box was about to be opened.

'Jackie? You know her, then?'

Mary found herself floundering. She wasn't used to lying so was having great difficulty in thinking something up to extricate herself from this explosive situation.

'Well, Auntie? Who is she?'

Mary still could not speak the words which she knew would break Joanie's heart. Oh, why couldn't I keep my big mouth shut!

'I'm waiting, Auntie.' Joanie was standing, hands on hips, her chin jutting out just like she sometimes did as a child when she'd felt an unjust grievance against her. Then it could be resolved with a cuddle and a kiss.

Now, it appeared that nothing could make this situation better. Best to tell her, she thought, she's probably thinking the worst anyway.

'She's Martin's fiancée. I just heard Henry say.' She moved towards her niece, seeing the impact this news was having on her. 'Oh, my dear,' she said, arms outstretched, 'I am so sorry.'

Joanie backed away, shaking her head as she did so.

She ran along the corridor and out into the hospital car park. It was still dark, which she was glad of, as it would hide both her and the tears that were spilling down her cheeks.

Once inside her car, she leant forward and, cupping her face in her hands, sobbed uncontrollably for several minutes. She cried for her mother, lying, for all intents and purposes, lifeless in her hospital bed.

She cried because she knew there was every possibility of their never becoming reconciled to one another, that her mother would leave her for good without ever telling her what Joanie, all her life, had wanted to hear her say — that she did, in fact, love her.

But her tears also fell for her own, more personal, heartache regarding Martin. Why did I ever allow him to make me feel as I still do about him? She knew there was no future for them but it still didn't stop her wishing with all her heart that there might have been.

And now this final humiliation when it seemed that everybody — even her aunt — knew that Martin had not just a girlfriend, but that she was his fiancée; not only knew but even knew her name.

★ ★ ★

Paula continued along the corridor. She had felt intimidated by the look that girl — Joanie? — had given her as she'd passed. I suppose she must have recognised me that day I went to her shop, she thought, and then dismissed her from her mind.

Far more important was how her father was. His wife did not merit much consideration on her part. She was only here because she had to be, no matter how much she resented her father remarrying after deserting their mother.

But it's true what they say, you put all these things aside when they're ill.

She came to the ward and saw both her father and her brother at Celia's bedside. Despite the hostile feelings she'd harboured, compassion and pity now swelled her heart.

Both Henry and Martin turned to see Paula enter the room. Martin, already standing, moved towards her approaching figure.

'How are you, Dad?' she asked, after a brief hug with her brother.

Henry smiled weakly.

'I'm fine, my dear. I got off lightly.'

'Doesn't look like it to me.' Paula frowned, looking all the time at Henry.

'Well, I am. It's your stepmother who bore the brunt of it.'

Martin hastily intervened.

'Father's doing well. Broken leg, a few fractured ribs, but generally OK.'

Paula now did actually look across at Celia — this woman whose existence she had, till now, thoroughly resented, and she found that, despite everything, she did feel a sort of pity for her, but only in the same way as she might have felt sympathy for a victim of an earthquake on the news; she was somehow able to remain detached from the full emotional consequences of this whole dreadful situation.

'Will she die, do you think?'

'Paula!' Martin hissed.

'Well, what have they said?'

Henry held out his hand towards his daughter, but she did not accept it.

'They can't say,' he told her. 'They just don't know.'

Martin hurriedly intervened, putting himself between father and daughter.

'She's hanging in there. On the positive side, she's young . . . ish. She's got every chance of getting through this. The doctors here know their stuff.'

'And yet,' Paula persisted, 'they can't tell you if she'll live or die.'

'They can't know everything, but they're doing their best, dear,' Henry intervened, desperate to believe that that was true.

They all seemed to be in a terrible sort of limbo, where no-one appeared able to change anything. It was all in the hands of fate.

'Let's see if we can get a drink, Paula,' Martin suggested, anxious for her not to add any further to Henry's fears. For a moment she remained where she stood, as if she had not heard him, but finally she turned away and followed Martin out into the corridor.

'You shouldn't say such things,' he admonished his younger sister, as they walked together. And yet, he was not altogether surprised by her response.

Younger than Martin by three years, she had always had this sort of direct manner with people. In truth it was her own, almost naïve honesty that, throughout her life, had got her into trouble.

In many ways he loved her for it — that was how she was, and he held a grudging admiration for her. But, of course, even in these enlightened times, it was not the best way to speak to people, especially when they were in this sort of situation, where the fear of death was on everyone's mind.

'I just wanted to know what her chances were, that's all.' Paula shrugged.

'We all do but the only people who can tell us are the medical staff, and they're just not sure yet. We must just keep hoping.'

'Sorry.' She leant against her brother as they walked, whilst he now put his arm around her. It was like this that they walked past the glass door entrance to the hospital which separated one corridor from another, just as Joanie, having wiped the tears from her eyes and blown her nose, looked across to see them go by.

So that's Jackie. She's the one he's been with all the time. He just used me and now he has the cheek to parade her in my face! Look at him, he just doesn't care!

181

Hello, Goodbye

Simon Reeds was struggling to find his socks. Every other part of his body was covered, just not his feet. He eventually discovered the pair under the bed and hastily retrieved them. From the bathroom he could hear the shower working. He looked at his watch. Nine-forty! He needed to get moving. And so did she.

'Jackie!' he bellowed.

$\star$ $\star$ $\star$

Mary had found Joanie, still sitting in her car, head down, unable to think of anything but what she had witnessed earlier.

Mary tapped gently on the car window, a smile at the ready for her niece when she responded, which she did now, offering a smaller, sadder smile than the one she was receiving.

Joanie unwound the window.

'Any news?' she asked.

'No. No change. I just wondered

where you were.'

'Well, here I am.' Joanie shrugged.

'Are you coming back in? It seems rather chilly out here.'

Joanie grabbed her handbag from the passenger seat.

'OK,' she said. Mary stepped back as she opened the car door. They then began walking silently back towards the hospital entrance.

'I'm sorry you had to hear from me about Martin. But I truly had no idea. I didn't even know he was Henry's son till a little while ago.'

'It really doesn't matter, Auntie,' Joanie replied, and she almost believed herself. In the time since she'd seen Martin and the girl Jackie go by — him with his arm around her — she felt that it had made her finally come to her senses, had hardened her heart.

Nothing would ever hurt her like he had again, she wouldn't let it. From now on her life would focus on her own needs and desires, and not let anyone else have any influence in it.

But that was a resolution for the coming New Year. For now there was still her mother to consider and worry over.

Mary offered her arm to her niece, which she took as they entered the hospital once more. There seemed to be more people about now. It had been light for a while, and shifts had changed.

'What about your shop, Joanie?' Mary asked, as they walked down the corridor.

'I really can't think of that at the moment, Auntie. How could I?'

'I just thought it might help to have something to occupy yourself with. Besides, all we are doing here is just waiting, there's nothing we can actually do.'

Joanie considered this. It would save her the embarrassment — humiliation — of continually bumping into Martin and his fiancée, reminding her of what an idiot she had been, how gullible, naïve, how utterly foolish to have allowed her heart to rule her head.

'I'll come in and see if there's been any change, and then perhaps I will go along to the shop.'

'I think that's a good idea. It will give you something else to think about.'

Henry was asleep in his wheelchair beside the bed where Celia lay, still sleeping herself, it would seem. A nurse was also in the room, checking the connected equipment and taking Celia's temperature.

She gave Joanie and Mary a brief, cursory nod, not saying anything as she left the room. Aunt and niece stood together, just inside the doorway, not wishing to go any further in case they disturbed Henry who, even in sleep, looked troubled.

Celia was still unconscious, looking no different from when they first arrived at the hospital several hours ago.

It struck Joanie that this whole scenario was like some sort of bizarre and cruel tapestry of life. Here there was her mother, whose life hung in the balance, with Henry, her husband only able to be a spectator to these events.

And here was she, beset by other factors beyond this possible tragedy, with Martin and his girlfriend, Jackie, haunting her with their transient presence.

Mary walked Joanie to her car.

'What will you do, Auntie? You look as if you could do with a rest.'

'I'm fine, dear. I believe they have a cafeteria here which should be open now. I expect I'll get myself a cup of coffee and a bite to eat.' She put her hand on Joanie's arm. 'You just make sure to drive safely, and see if you can get some sleep yourself at home.'

Home? Joanie couldn't immediately associate anywhere with home just at present. She felt like she was drifting from one unconnected thing to another. Even the prospect of going to work seemed almost surreal in the circumstances.

'Ring me if there's any change, won't you?'

'Of course I will.' Mary watched Joanie drive off, before turning back to re-enter the building.

Martin was coming out of the entrance as Mary approached. He stood back to let her pass, which she did, and would have continued on her way had he not called out to her.

'What is it, Martin?' she said, in a tone not intended to encourage any dialogue between them.

'Can we talk, Mary? I need to explain.'

'Explain what, exactly?' Mary was not prepared to allow this young man, who had caused her niece so much heartache, to feel he had any right to her counsel. She'd felt betrayed, too.

'Could we just go somewhere? I really do need you to hear me out.'

In the end Mary agreed. She couldn't be as heartless as she considered Martin to be, although she began to doubt both her and Joanie's swift judgement on him.

Nevertheless, what could not be denied was that he was now engaged to be married, and that it was rubbing salt into the wound to have brought his fiancée to the hospital.

They were seated opposite one another in the busy public cafeteria, a cup of coffee each. Mary focused all her attention on her cup, stirring needlessly its frothy contents, waiting for Martin to speak. Finally, as the silence continued, she looked up into his anguished face.

'Well?'

'I've been trying to work out where to begin,' he said, smiling awkwardly.

'Well, you know what they say — the beginning's usually the best place.'

Again he smiled, but once more it seemed a reflex gesture, trying to conceal what he was really feeling.

'I've made a right mess of things — of everything. I love your niece, Mary, but somehow I lost her through my own stupid fault.'

Mary interrupted him.

'How can you say you love Joanie and then go and get engaged to someone else? It's both cruel and ridiculous.'

'I know, I know. But when we met at your sister's wedding neither of us had any idea that we were related by law due to their marriage.'

'I don't understand.'

Martin frowned.

'Didn't Joanie tell you?'

'Tell me what?'

Martin recounted the whole scenario that took place at Celia's front door on the day of the wedding reception.

Mary was confused.

'But Henry's name is Smythe — you're Smith.'

Martin nodded.

'I really didn't think it mattered. When I was at school I was ribbed something rotten by my classmates over being called Smythe. That's why, at the first opportunity I called myself Smith — it seemed less pretentious. But it was only a small thing — I hadn't changed my identity completely like Joanie obviously had.'

Mary couldn't argue with that, so continued to listen to Martin as his story unravelled.

'You'd better go and find her,' was all she could say when he'd finished. 'She's probably at her shop.' She hoped that she'd made the right decision.

★ ★ ★

Martin, however, did not go immediately to A La Mod. Instead he took Paula back to their mother's and then went to his own place. He felt he needed to change. The hospital and all its clinical odours seemed to have permeated his clothes and his body. A quick shower and a fresh outfit helped to give him both the courage and — to a lesser extent — the confidence to face Joanie.

He was just about to leave when he heard the phone ringing.

Nervous, and a little afraid, he lifted the receiver. What he heard came as an immense relief, spurring him on to do what he felt he had to do.

But once he was behind the wheel of his sports car, and getting ever closer to his destination, his nerve almost failed him.

Every time he came to a red traffic light he took it as a sign that he himself should stop and turn around. After all, what good would it do, even if she accepted the truth of his story? But at least, now, he was free of one particular problem . . . She could no longer use that as a weapon against him.

The fact that he thought in terms of weaponry indicated to him what a probable mountain he was going to have to climb in order to regain Joanie's trust and, hopefully, her love. These conflicting thoughts continued to torment him as he continued on his way to A La Mod.

On arrival, Martin decided to park in a side road. He wasn't sure why, it just seemed the safest option. He then walked purposefully along the road till he came to the door of Joanie's shop. It was here he very nearly lost his nerve. He could just see Joanie at her counter, looking down at an item of clothing. She hadn't seen him.

Turn around, a voice in his head said. She won't want to see you, or listen to your pathetic excuses. He knew this very likely to be true, but if he didn't find out for himself he could spend the rest of his life wondering what might have been.

He entered the shop. As the door pinged Joanie looked up.

'Hello,' was all Martin could manage to say, his throat was suddenly so very dry.

Joanie gave him a look that told him, without the need for words, what she thought of his coming here.

'Goodbye,' she said.

Baby, Now That I've Found You

Martin stood in the doorway, determined, now that he was here, not to turn and run. Even through the hostility showing in Joanie's eyes — directed at him — he could see why he had fallen in love with her.

Now, since his father's revelation, there could be no obstacle, socially, for them not to be together, this time for ever. However, that was the future, hopefully. First of all he had to deal with the here and now, and things did not look promising.

'I have to talk to you, Joanie. Please hear me out. I've been a fool, I know, but I need you to know the truth.'

'Truth!' Joanie sneered. 'Where and when did truth come into all of this? And does your fiancée, Jackie, know that you're here, wanting to tell me the truth?'

Despite her sneering sarcasm, Martin felt some small measure of hope. She was actually speaking to him, never mind that, so far, she hadn't had a good word to say.

At least she hadn't told him to get out. She was standing facing him, both hands on the counter, actually waiting — hoping — for an explanation that might make it possible for them to begin again, but she wasn't holding her breath.

'Can I come in?' Martin asked. Joanie did not respond so, taking this also as a good sign, he stepped further into the shop.

'Turn the sign,' Joanie told him.

'Sign?'

Joanie pointed impatiently to the *Open/Closed* sign that hung on the door. Martin turned it round.

'Now push the bolt across.' He did so, then awaited any further instruction. 'Well?' she said, not prepared to give any ground.

'Do you think we might go out the back to talk? It seems a bit public here — and strange.' As soon as he said this he immediately regretted it.

Surprisingly, though, Joanie moved away from the counter and, without saying anything, went through to the back room. More surprisingly, she put the kettle on. Martin mutely followed. He stood awkwardly in the room, not liking — or daring — to sit down yet.

'I've forgotten, do you take sugar?' Joanie asked, even though she knew perfectly well that he didn't.

'No, er, no, thanks.'

There followed what seemed like an endless silence only broken by the sound of the kettle heating up. Eventually the coffee was made. Joanie placed Martin's mug on the opposite side of the worktable to where Joanie now placed herself. He waited nervously for her to be seated before he sat down himself.

'This is lovely coffee,' he said, by way of an opener.

Joanie did not respond. She was as anxious as him to get to the point — to come up with some credible reason for what had happened, something that might make it possible for them to be a couple again. But it was hard to imagine what that could be.

First of all, Martin apologised for his behaviour at the wedding reception, his only excuse being that he could not understand why Joanie seemed to be known by two, totally different, names.

Joanie explained, then countered with her own incomprehension concerning Martin's surname. Now he explained. So that at least was clear.

'But what does any of this matter?' Joanie sighed. 'You're engaged to be married to the lovely Jackie.' Unknowingly, she was picturing Paula when she said it. And, at the moment, Martin did not realise her mistaken identity.

His eyes lit up. Here, surely, there was hope, having the news that he'd heard earlier to offer her. But, just as he was about to tell her, the telephone rang. Joanie sprang to her feet and dashed to the phone. As she answered, she was breathing as rapidly as if she'd had had to run a mile to get to it.

'Hello. Yes, speaking.' There was a long pause as the person on the other end of the line conveyed their message. Martin assumed, from the look on Joanie's face, that it must be the hospital she was talking to.

'I'll come right away,' Joanie said, hanging up. She turned to Martin. 'I have to go, that was the hospital.'

Martin leapt from his chair.

'I'll take you, my car's just around the corner.'

Joanie frowned.

'And my car's just outside. Are you coming or what?'

They both got into her car which took off at speed.

'What did they say?' he dared to ask, a mile along the road.

'They said she's showing signs of cognitive recovery, whatever that means.'

'That's good, surely. Anything else. Is she conscious?'

'No, but her eyelids were flickering and her hands were moving slightly. Oh,

Martin, I do hope she's going to recover.'

Martin reached across and covered Joanie's hand with his, which she did not shrink from, even though there was no other acknowledgement.

* * *

They had no sooner arrived at the hospital and parked than Joanie was out of her car and hurrying towards the main entrance. As she was about to go in she turned and called out to Martin.

'Don't bring her in!' And then she vanished.

Martin didn't know what Joanie meant by that. He also wondered whether he should follow her in. After all, it wasn't his mother. But then he recognised that his father might welcome his support.

Why does it seem that there are two opposing sides in all this, he wondered, as he made his own way, at a slower place towards the ward.

The corridors were a whole lot busier now. He checked his watch. Twenty to eleven.

Joanie found Henry still exactly where he had been when she'd last been in here. Also in the room was her aunt. She looked totally drained but put on a brave face as her niece walked in.

'Anything?' Joanie asked. 'They phoned me and said she might wake up.'

Henry looked round at her.

'We're hoping so, but they have no idea how long that might take.' He, too, looked tired but his eyes were shining with an expression of hope and optimism. They all shared that same feeling, as they looked down intently at Celia.

And, as they were watching, her eyelids did flicker, and continued to flicker until suddenly her eyes opened and she was staring wildly at the ceiling.

Henry stretched across until he was immediately above Celia's wide-eyed face.

'Hello, darling, it's me.'

Celia's face shone like the sun clearing a cloud.

'Oh, Edward, my dear,' she managed

to say, trying to raise an arm with which to hug him.

Henry frowned, bewildered.

'No, my darling, it's me, Henry.'

'I knew you'd come back, I always knew. I never believed them when they said you'd been killed.' Her eyes brightened even more as she went on.

'And I have news, my dear, such wonderful news. We have a beautiful baby daughter. I named her Jean. She is just like a delicate little flower. Just wait till you see her, you'll love her, too.'

'I'd better find the doctor,' Mary said as, with tears running down her cheeks, she hurried out of the room.

Henry, a look of deep anguish on his face, turned to Joanie.

'Was Edward your father?'

Joanie, too choked up to speak, simply nodded.

Henry put his head in his hands and groaned. Joanie continued to look at her mother, seeing for the first time a person whose heart was full of love — for her, as well as for her dead husband. It was a beautiful yet tragic moment.

The doctor entered the room, followed by his trusty nurse.

'If you could give us a moment, please,' he said to the assembled group before turning his attention to Celia. The nurse, simply by using her eyes — like a sheepdog might — encouraged everyone to leave.

In the corridor, Henry, addressed no-one in particular.

'What can this mean? Does she really not know who I am?'

Nobody had an answer to that. They just hoped that the doctor, when he came out, would be able to offer a rational explanation. Joanie, still feeling astonished at seeing her mother showing so much emotion, found herself unable to look Henry in the eye. Instead she turned her face towards the corridor at the same time as Martin approached, and he wasn't alone!

'What's happened?' Martin asked.

Joanie continued to stare at the young woman beside Martin, unable to believe the nerve of them both.

Mary spoke for them.

'She's awake, but a little confused.'

'A little?' Henry said, flabbergasted. 'What does that mean?'

Joanie was astounded by the cheek of this . . . Jackie. It had nothing to do with her, yet here she was, poking her nose in where it had no business to be. Before she could think of something to say that might put her well and truly in her place the doctor and the nurse came out to speak to them.

'Well?' Henry demanded. 'Why didn't she recognise me?'

The doctor looked kindly on them all, but Henry in particular.

'It's not altogether unusual in these circumstances, given the trauma she's experienced. From a medical point of view it's a good sign. I appreciate that it must have come as a shock — particularly for you, Mr Smythe — but please be assured that, as the swelling goes down, we fully expect her term memory to put itself in its correct order.'

'Can we go back and see her?' Joanie asked, afraid that her mother might revert back to her former — usual — cool indifference. She wanted a chance to experience her affection first hand, if possible.

'Yes, you may.' The doctor smiled. 'But try not to excite her. She needs to remain as calm as possible, but I'm sure she'll be pleased to see you all.'

'Except me,' Henry muttered.

The nurse heard what Henry had said and moved forward to speak to him.

'You mustn't take it personally,' she told him. 'As the doctor says, we have every hope that she'll get better.'

The doctor moved off without another word, leaving the nurse to try to catch up, as usual.

'Shall we go in, Joanie?' Mary said, sensing a charged atmosphere building up out here in the corridor.

'Yes, Auntie.' As everyone began to move towards the door, Joanie stepped in front of Martin, and nodded towards his sister.

'Family only,' she said.

'She is family,' Martin told her.

'I don't think so,' Joanie insisted. 'You haven't married her yet.'

'Would someone tell me what's going on?' Paula asked. 'Because I haven't a clue.'

'Don't give me that, Jackie . . . '

Before Joanie could say any more, Paula, angry herself now, hit back.

'Who are you calling Jackie? My name's Paula.'

'Yes,' Martin said, 'and she's my sister.'

'Your sister? You never said you had a sister! What else don't I know about you?' And with that she turned on her heel and walked back to join her aunt in the IT room.

Paula looked up at her elder brother.

'What's going on, Marty?' she wanted to know.

'It's a long story, but now's not the time for explanations.'

Celia Smythe was still lying back, although the head frame of her bed had

204

been raised a little, in order that she would be better able to see her visitors. And the first one her eyes lit on was Joanie.

Raising her arms slightly — trying to beckon — she was able to persuade her daughter to come towards her, which Joanie now did, both with anticipation and fear.

'Jean, my darling girl,' Celia whispered, tears of joy filling her eyes. Joanie took her hand, tears welling up in her own eyes. 'You have grown into a beautiful young woman.'

It seemed that her mother's mind was swinging to and fro like a pendulum, where one moment she was back in the 1940s and the next she was in the present day.

The doctor had said that this could happen, and would continue to do so until — or if — the swelling on her brain had returned to its normal size. This worried Joanie. She didn't want things, however they panned out, to return to how they had been for all her life so far.

But at the same time, she was over-joyed at her mother's open display of love and affection towards her. It made up, in some ways, for the disappointments of her own, regarding her love life.

At least, for now, the one who really mattered, had expressed love for her only child.

Love is All Around

Everyone, except Henry, had gone off to stretch their legs or get something to eat or drink. Joanie decided to go and sit in her car; it had become her refuge. Also, she needed the quiet space to try to make sense of all the things going on in her head. Her aunt had told her to take encouragement from what had happened.

'It shows, Joanie, that deep down she's always loved you,' she said.

'Try telling that to poor Henry,' Joanie replied, feeling both pity for her mother's husband and concern that all of this might just be a temporary blip and that, eventually, her mother's seemingly natural personality would return.

All of a sudden she felt ravenously hungry. She looked at her watch. Nine-fifty. What day was it? She was losing all track of time. Everything was all so up in the air.

She decided, finally, after sitting for a little while longer, to drive back to

Chepswell, buy a sandwich at the deli and then get back into some sort of recognisable — normal — routine.

She had already started up the engine and was about to set off when she saw Paula striding purposefully towards her. For an instant Joanie was tempted to not meet her eye and drive off but there was something in the girl's expression which made her stay.

She wound down her window. Paula's pace had slowed considerably the nearer she got. And the look on her face was one of contrition.

'I think I owe you an apology,' she said, leaning in towards Joanie's open window.'

'I was thinking the same,' Joanie said. 'I mean, I ought to apologise to you,' she quickly added.

Paula frowned, looking puzzled.

'Look, I don't know about you,' Joanie said, 'but I'm starving. I was just about to go off and have a bite to eat. What say you come, too?'

'Really?' Paula said. Joanie reached

across and opened the passenger door. In a few minutes they were heading in the direction of Chepswell.

In the end, though, they stopped at a Wimpy bar as they were able to park virtually outside it.

'You find a table and I'll order for us. What d'you fancy?'

'Just a coffee, please,' Paula said. She found a table near the large plate glass window. Joanie brought the tray over and handed Paula her coffee. She then sat down with her own meal.

After a few minutes of concentrated eating and drinking, Joanie, wiping her lips and fingers with the paper napkin, looked across at the girl opposite.

'So you're Martin's sister. I had no idea.'

'Didn't Marty mention me at all?'

'There was never time for that. Looking back, I see we never really got to know each other at all.'

'I know he loves you,' Paula said.

Joanie's mug was halfway to her lips when Paula said this. She gently lowered it back on to the Formica topped table, but continued to hold on to it because her hands — like her heart — were starting to tremble.

'How can you say that?'

'Because all he ever talked about to me was you. I'm younger than Marty by just over three years. I've always looked up to him — he's a sort of hero to me.

'So, when he started going on about you it made me kind of jealous, if you can understand . . .'

'It's all right, Paula. I know now it was you who came to my shop that day, when I was closed, and I asked you if you wanted to come inside. You weren't interested in my stock — you wanted to have a good look at me.'

Joanie said this, not with malice but with relief, as if she'd suddenly been able to solve a riddle.

'I'm afraid so. I just wanted to see for myself who this wonderful girl was who had her own shop, designed her own clothes, and who seemed absolutely perfect.'

'Well, as you can see, I'm just an ordinary girl, trying to make my way in the world. But it hardly matters now, anyway. Martin's got engaged to this Jackie.'

Paula shook her head.

'I had no idea things had gone that far. Yes, they went out a few times, after you dumped him . . .'

'I didn't dump him!' Joanie was quite indignant.

'Well, anyway, when you and Marty stopped going out together, Jackie suddenly appeared on the scene. They work together, that's how they knew each other.

'But I was a bit surprised at his choice. They're like chalk and cheese with nothing really in common except their jobs. But I had no idea they'd got engaged — he never said anything.'

This surprised Joanie and, absurdly, gave her a faint sense of hope. Surely if you got engaged you'd want to celebrate, to share your happy news with everyone. It was all a bit strange. But then maybe that was how Martin really was — secretive, private.

There seemed no point in pursuing this line of conversation any more, so Joanie let it drop.

'So, what do you do for a living, Paula?' she asked, trying to lighten the mood.

'I work in an estate agent's . . . clerk, typist, that sort of thing.'

'Oh, that must be interesting.'

'In what way?' Paula had a look on her face as if she thought Joanie was being sarcastic, which she certainly wasn't.

'Well, I mean, I imagine seeing all the different people coming in, looking for all various types of property. I'd be working out what they could afford or want by what clothes they were wearing.'

Paula grinned.

'It's true, I do that. But you'd be surprised, sometimes. People come in off the street looking like they've been dragged through a hedge backwards and then they pay cash for a Georgian mansion with stables and acres of land.'

'Probably pop stars. Where exactly is your branch?'

'Henrietta Place, just off Oxford Street. Do you know it?'

'I know Henrietta Place, yes.' Another piece of the jigsaw fell into place. The puzzle was gradually piecing together. But, she knew there would never be a complete picture to all this because neither she or Martin would be in it.

* * *

Martin had had to walk some distance before finding a telephone box. He just hoped that Jackie would be on the other end of the line to answer it. End of the line. He could almost smile at the analogy but it never showed on his face which was set in a look of steely determination.

'Hello?'

'Jackie?'

'Is that you, Martin?'

'Yes.'

A short silence ensued whilst Jackie planned her strategies.

'Well, I haven't changed my mind, if that's what you're hoping. Simon and I

213

are going to get married.'

'I'm very pleased for you both, really I am.'

'You are?' There was almost a hint of disappointment in Jackie's voice. She had been hoping that Martin — like all her previous exes — would be absolutely devastated by her rejection. This was something new. 'What do you want, then?

I don't imagine for one minute you've telephoned just to give me your blessing.'

'Not exactly, no, although I am genuinely pleased for you both . . . ' And me, he thought. 'No, I just wanted to let you know you can keep the ring. I won't be wanting it back, OK?'

Jackie, with her over-inflated ego, took this to mean that Martin would never again have any need for an engagement ring — that his life from now on would be like that of a celibate monk.

She was rather pleased, mainly because the ring was worth a bit of money, something Simon Reeds need not know about.

However, she wasn't going to tell Martin of the pleasurable satisfaction his news gave her. Certainly not.

'I should think so, too,' she said, affecting an injured tone in her voice. 'I shall always keep it, Martin — something to remind me of what might have been.'

Unknown to Martin, she brought her lips even closer to the mouthpiece and sighed heavily, hoping it would make him feel even worse.

'There's a funny noise on the line, I've got to go. Bye, Jackie, enjoy your life.' Before she could respond, he hung up.

That's one problem solved, he thought, but knowing that didn't bring him much comfort. Only one thing would and he wasn't sure that he had a right to wish for it.

★ ★ ★

Mary was still at the hospital, as was Henry. He looked as if he hadn't slept in ages. She felt a great wave of pity for him. Poor man. I don't know what I can say or do to make him feel better. I'm as confused as everyone else.

She thought about Ray and wondered if it would be possible now for him and his son and daughter to come over for Christmas. Everything was in a muddle, not least her poor sister's brain.

They'd removed some of the tubes and there was talk of putting her on one of the wards, which was good news, meaning she was probably out of danger. The next few days would be crucial, but all the signs were promising. Whether that meant she would fully recover from her injuries was another matter.

Henry, despite his fatigue and worries concerning his wife's mental state, was due to be discharged today which gave Mary an idea.

'I think you should come and stay with me till you're more mobile,' she told him.

'I couldn't possibly,' he said, but there was a definite lack of conviction in his voice.

'I insist. Apart from anything else you shouldn't be on your own right now. You need people — friendly people — around you.

'Besides, the district nurse and your own doctor will be coming round to check up on you.

'Celia's going to be here for another week at least, so you can't just hang around here indefinitely. Let's not hear any more about it, you're coming home with me.'

And so it was arranged.

An ambulance was booked to take both Henry and Mary back to her house where she quickly made up a bed in the downstairs sitting-room, with help from the two ambulance people who were happy to carry one of the two single beds down the wide staircase.

She tried to give them a tip but they wouldn't hear of it.

Someone from the hospital would be coming shortly to see what other things Henry might need for his stay. He had already retained the wheelchair plus a pair of crutches. He intended to be as independent as it was possible to be with a leg in plaster, and Mary secretly admired his stoicism.

Afterwards, she went through the mail.

Amongst the usual assortment of bills was an airmail envelope from France. From Ray.

She almost held her breath as she opened it, fearing more bad news.

She'd not yet had time to write to him and tell of her own news, not since the accident, but there was no reason to think — logically — that just because things had been going wrong here that they would also be doing so across the Channel.

So it was a relief to read how much he and his children were looking forward to coming over.

'If you're sure it will be no trouble. My son has visited England when he was doing his agricultural studies but Yvette has never travelled further than Paris, so it will be very exciting for her.'

Mary continued reading the rest of Ray's letter, a smile setting on her face as she did so. When she'd finished she felt a great surge of warmth engulf her, and considered herself very fortunate to be having Ray and his family come and stay.

* * *

Martin sat pensively on the edge of his bed. He felt he was at a crossroads and he wanted to be sure to take the right turning, and not end up in no man's land where his future would look decidedly bleak and lonely.

He desperately wanted to see Joanie, to explain everything to her, to make her love him again as he had not stopped loving her.

But, at the hospital, she was nowhere to be found, neither was his sister.

Not knowing what to do, he thought it best to come home and try to work out the best course of action.

If Joanie wasn't at the hospital the chances were she was at her shop. Should he go there again? It was very unlikely that she would be pleased to see him.

Apart from anything else she had a business to run, one that depended very heavily on sales right now to see her through the leaner winter months of the new year.

He also had a job of his own to maintain. He couldn't keep asking for time off on compassionate grounds, especially as his father was due to be discharged later today.

That was something else he had to give thought to. Obviously Henry wouldn't be able to go back to Setford Avenue — not on his own — unless he himself should go and stay there with him, for the time being, at least.

But even as he thought it he knew Joanie wouldn't be best pleased about it, even though it had never, as far as she could remember, ever been her family home.

He sighed. Families! How they complicate our lives.

I'm Coming Home

Joanie was giving Paula a full tour of her premises which, obviously, was only taking as long as the kettle took to boil. She had discovered that today was actually Monday so her shop wouldn't have been open anyway.

She was rather glad of that because it gave her the time to get to know Paula better, even though it might make it awkward as far as Martin was concerned. But, actually, she no longer cared whether it mattered or not. Too often she had taken other people's feelings into account instead of her own, and where had it got her?

'Did you design all these clothes?' Paula asked, going from rail to rail.

Joanie smiled.

'Not all, no. I'd never fill the shop if I depended on stocking it exclusively with my own designs, but I mix mine in, and some of my regular customers do come in just to buy what I have made.'

'Wow, that must make you feel good.'

'It does, actually, yes.'

'Is this one of yours?' Paula had taken a jacket and matching skirt from one of the rails she'd been looking through. It was a deep purple colour, made of velvet cotton.

'Yes, that's mine. There's a hat to go with it as well.'

'It's beautiful.' Paula was running her hands over the material, stroking it as if it were a living thing.

Joanie had an idea.

'I think you'd look great in it. Why don't you try it on while I go look for the hat?'

Paula looked uneasy.

'I couldn't possibly. I don't have that sort of money to buy something like this.' She began hastily, to put the outfit back onto the rail.

'Oh, please,' Joanie said. 'Humour me. It's one of my latest designs and I just wanted to see what it looked like on someone. You've got just the right figure to show it off at its best.

'Plus it will give me a chance to see what accessories would go well with it. Go on, the changing room's just over there. Put it on while I find the hat that goes with it.'

Joanie's skills as a salesperson as well as a fashion designer had their effect on Paula who quickly retrieved the outfit from the rail and set off to the changing room — an alcove with a curtain — whilst Joanie went to find the matching hat.

When Paula drew back the curtain and stepped out into the shop, the transformation was truly amazing. Joanie stood still, hat in hand, feeling quite emotional by what she saw. Paula was a beautiful young woman who, till now it seemed, had never really worn the clothes that best set off her looks and figure.

'How do I look?' Paula asked, grinning.
'How do you look!' Joanie responded. 'You look beautiful, absolutely beautiful.'

'It's an amazing outfit. I feel really good in it.'

'And so you should.' Joanie walked over to Paula and placed the fedora style hat gently on the young woman's head. 'Go and look in the mirror. See what you think.'

Paula did as Joanie suggested, making just the tiniest of adjustments to the hat as she studied herself in the mirror. The smile she'd had earlier was still there, and Joanie felt both pleased and proud for them both.

But then Paula's smile suddenly vanished as she stepped away from the mirror and came over to Joanie. Taking the hat off, she spoke without meeting Joanie's eyes.

'Thanks for letting me try these on. I should be getting home now, otherwise Mum will start wondering where I am.'

It was as though she was Cinderella, back in her rags. Joanie could see that she was embarrassed, so came up with an idea.

'You don't work Saturdays, do you?' Paula shook her head, frowning, puzzled.

'Every year,' Joanie went on, 'I tell myself I could do with some help in the shop, and every year it never happens. What I'm proposing, Paula, is that you come and work for me for a few hours during the two busiest Saturdays leading up to Christmas. I'll pay you, of course, but I'll also give you this outfit as part payment, if that's all right with you.'

Paula's eyes lit up.

'Are you serious?'

'Of course I am. And what else I'd like you to do is wear one or two of my other winter designs to give people an idea of just how fabulous they look.'

And so it was agreed. And to celebrate the deal, Joanie made them both a mug of coffee and opened a packet of chocolate digestives.

Afterwards, she wrapped Paula's new outfit and put it into one of her A La Mod carrier bags, and then drove her, through the darkening evening, the couple of miles or so to Paula's mother's house, a quite grand, mock Tudor detached villa in the sleepy suburbs of

Primrose Hill.

'Lovely house,' Joanie remarked, as Paula got out of the car, although there was an air of dark melancholy about it.

Other properties had lit up Christmas trees in their windows, and there were lights also on some of the trees in various gardens. Paula's mother's house looked rather joyless by comparison.

As if reading Joanie's mind, Paula leant back in.

'Mum doesn't really go in much for Christmas,' she said. 'She says it's lost its meaning.'

Joanie smiled sympathetically.

'It is a very nice house, Paula. I'll see you on Saturday, around eleven. That's when it starts to get busy.'

'Great. What shall I wear, this?' She held up the carrier bag with the purple outfit in it.

'Yes, please. It's going to make all the difference. See you.' And she drove off.

★　★　★

226

It was just over a fortnight to Christmas. Celia, improving rapidly, had been moved on to a ward. She still had moments of confusion but, generally speaking, her mind was recovering well. She now remembered who Henry was.

She knew they'd been in a car accident but could recall nothing about it. She could also remember that her daughter, Jean, had been at the hospital.

Jean, my daughter, who I gave up.

Thinking of this made her cry, it was so sad. She found it impossible to believe, or accept, that she had done such a thing, but she also knew that she had.

Henry visited every day. He seemed to need to reassure himself that Celia was not only getting better but was recognising that it was he, Henry, who was here to see her. Henry, her husband. And it appeared to work.

She never referred to him as Edward again, and his persistence at being by her side whenever he could, and in spite of the physical difficulties involved in getting to see her, was paying off. There was not only the look of recognition on her face, but also the look of love, which was of huge benefit to them both on their, now shared, road to recovery.

Joanie still remained apprehensive when coming to see her mother, so chose to always go along when her aunt was also visiting.

Her apprehension was not only confined to seeing her mother, though. She was afraid that her visits would also coincide with Martin's who, as often as was possible with his flight rotas, would bring his father to the hospital — not in his sports car, of course, but in a taxi.

However, it never happened and so, day by day, like a dripping tap, her feelings for him seemed to be wearing away.

Celia, much to Joanie's relief and surprise, continued to be pleased to see her daughter. It was as if the accident had had a jolting effect on her emotions, like when you bang the top of a TV that's playing up and suddenly the picture is back.

She was often tearful, though — contrite, guilt-ridden. But Joanie wanted none of that. She was just so glad to be meeting the mother she never knew she had.

'You will come and see me when I get home?' Celia was almost pleading with Joanie, holding on to her hand with ever increasing strength.

'Of course I will, Mum. I'd love to.'

Joanie saying and then Celia hearing the endearment 'Mum' brought tears to the eyes of both of them, but they smiled through the tears, growing ever more confident in their shared belief that things between them would always be better than good from now on.

If only it could be true of everything.

Celia's recovery had proved quicker than any of the specialist doctors had hoped, and so it was agreed that she could go home just in time for Christmas.

The problem was, with Henry settled in at her sister's, she would have been alone in her own house, and the doctors, had they known, would not have then agreed to her being discharged.

Joanie discussed the problem with her aunt, one Sunday morning, over coffee at her aunt's house. Like old times, although nothing, it seemed, would ever be the same again, and mostly for all the right reasons.

'Ideally, I'd like her to come here but I won't have the space once Ray and his children come,' Mary explained.

'It would be a shame for Mum and Henry not to be able to share their first Christmas together as husband and wife.'

'I know, but what can we do?'

Joanie suddenly had an idea. An idea that would give her an excuse to speak to Martin again.

All I Want for Christmas is You

It was to be a Christmas like no other. Joanie had, as she intended, telephoned Martin who, luckily was in.

'I think my mother and Henry should be allowed to spend Christmas together, don't you?'

'I do, yes. But I'm not sure how we're going to manage it.'

Joanie liked his use of the term 'we', it somehow brought them back together to some extent.

'Well, if you could help me get their beds downstairs and into the lounge then I'm sure it's possible.'

'Fine,' Martin said, 'but who's going to be there to look after them?'

'I've thought of that. I'm going to stay with them, cook them a Christmas dinner, and generally keep them happy if I can.'

'I'm sure you can. And, actually, I

should be back in town late Christmas Eve, so I could come over and give you a hand.'

'What about your mother, and Paula?'

There was a brief pause on the other end of the line.

'My mother won't be at home for Christmas. She's arranged to go and stay with a 'friend' for the holiday.'

The way he said the word 'friend' implied to Joanie that whoever it was, was probably more than just a friend.

'And Paula? What about her? Where will she be?' She surprised herself just how concerned she was for Paula's welfare.

Since she'd come to help Joanie in the shop they'd developed a bond very much as if they were sisters — very ironic seeing that they were stepsisters, in the legal sense. And, of course, that was a painful reminder that Martin was Joanie's stepbrother.

'I was going to stay with her at mother's house, although we haven't got anything in yet. But at least she won't be on her own.'

'I've got a better idea,' Joanie said, and she hoped she had.

*   *   *

Mary wondered how her niece was getting on, this being Christmas Day. She herself had been having a wonderful time. Henry had gone home, allowing Ray to make use of his temporary bed which both father and son, Jacques, had returned to the second bedroom where the two men would now sleep.

The Christmas dinner had been enjoyed by everyone and Yvette had kindly helped with the washing up.

The festive tree and all the other decorations had been put up by everyone, Ray and his family having arrived on the twenty-third.

Mary hadn't experienced a Christmas like this before and it was, to her mind, how it should be. It was just a shame that Joanie couldn't be with them on this day, although her niece had intrigued her when speaking on the phone this morning, to say she would be popping over later that afternoon with some news.

'Good news, I hope,' Mary had said, a bit cautious after all that had gone on before.

'Very good news, Auntie. Very good news indeed.'

All My Loving

Joanie, too, was having a wonderful time, as were her mother and Henry, and Paula and Martin who were sharing Christmas with them.

'A bit more pudding, Paula?'

'Oh, no, Joanie. Thank you, but I couldn't eat another thing. It was really delicious, though.'

'What about you, Martin? Could you manage any more?' Again the same response. 'I hoped you made a wish,' she added, smiling.

'I didn't have to,' he said, also smiling. 'My wish has already come true.'

Celia had, with the help of Joanie and Martin, gone upstairs for a lie down.

'I've had a wonderful time, my dear.' She smiled at her daughter, as she lowered herself gently on to the bed.

Henry was already asleep in the armchair with its footstool for comfort.

The three younger ones stayed at the table for a little while longer, chatting and laughing.

Joanie was thinking what fun it had been going round the local market with Paula, choosing all the food and decorations — including a magnificent tree. And now everyone was enjoying themselves as if all the troubles of the world had been lifted from their shoulders.

But, prior to all this, two days before, in fact, Martin had told her what Henry had said to him that the truth was that he wasn't actually Martin's father, even though, in every other respect, he looked upon him as his son.

'I don't want Paula to know,' he'd said, 'not at the moment, anyway. I don't want her upset unnecessarily.'

'I won't say anything.'

'Thank you.'

Martin and Joanie had been alone together in Joanie's workroom that day, whilst Paula was upstairs in the flat making it all look Christmassy, despite the fact that none of them would be spending much time there over the brief holiday.

The workroom was a bit of a mess

after these last few frantic shopping days. The shop had sold out of everything that Paula had worn. She had given all the outfits that extra touch of glamour and beauty. It had been a brilliant idea of Joanie's to get her to do it, and Paula was pleased, too.

After Martin had finished recounting Henry's story, as well as explaining that he and Jackie were no longer together, he'd continued to look at Joanie for some time. It might have been awkward had not Joanie been looking at him in much the same way.

Moments later they were in each other's arms, kissing with a passion and desire that their separation had deprived them of.

'I love you so much, Joanie,' Martin had said, as they slowly drew apart. 'I always have and I always will.'

'I love you too, Martin.'

They'd kissed again, and then Joanie spoke.

'No more secrets, Martin.'

'No more secrets.'

'I want everything to be what it seems.'

* * *

The wedding took place at 11 a.m. on April 6, at the Hillford register office, the same place Celia and Henry had married nearly a year before. It was a beautiful, sunny morning and simply a lovely day to get married.

Henry escorted Joanie, who was wearing a wedding outfit of her own design, the few steps forward to where the registrar and the keenly waiting groom stood.

Martin had dispensed with a best man. Instead, when Henry had completed his duty of giving away the bride, he neatly stepped across to stand beside Martin, the ring in his suit inner pocket.

There was no sign of any effects from his car accident; he was walking as well as before.

Celia, too, seated at the front alongside Paula and Sue, looked to have suffered no permanent damage.

There were occasional moments when

her memory lapsed but it didn't affect her newly recovered, affectionate persona.

Sue, despite — or probably because of — the occasion found herself constantly looking at and touching the engagement ring on her finger.

Anthony had asked her to marry him just a few days before, and she'd said yes. He hadn't tried to pressure her into living with him. He could tell that it wasn't what she wanted, and he loved her for it.

And she loved him back, although there were certain of his business practices that she was going to have to sort out — after the honeymoon!

Martin had invited his mother to the wedding but she declined, her excuse being that she and her 'friend' had already booked a holiday, coincidentally for the same date.

Martin shrugged; it was probably for the best, anyway.

Mary sat on the other side, just for the sake of balance. Next to her was Ray. Their fingers touched as they sat there.

A closeness had developed over Christmas and it was still growing.

Everything was such a contrast to the last time people were here. A happy day, which was just what it should be, just what it seemed.